THE HORSESHOE TRILOGIES

Charity's Gift

THE HORSESHOE TRILOGIES

Charity's Gift

by
Lucy Daniels

HYPERION
New York

Special thanks to Linda Chapman

Text copyright © 2004 by Working Partners Limited
Cover illustration copyright © 2004 by Tristan Elwell

The Horseshoe Trilogies and the Volo colophon are trademarks of Disney Enterprises, Inc.
Volo® is a registered trademark of Disney Enterprises, Inc.

Printed in the United States of America

First Edition, 2004
1 3 5 7 9 10 8 6 4 2

This book is set in 12.5-point Life Roman.
ISBN 0-7868-1752-6

Visit www.hyperionbooksforchildren.com

CHAPTER ONE

"Prepare to trot," announced Sally, the riding instructor at Lonsdale Stables. She waited until all four children had shortened their reins before calling out, "Trot on!"

Leaning against the gate of the school ring, Josie Grace pushed her auburn hair behind her ears and focused on the rider at the back. Six-year-old Ellie Carter was posting up and down in perfect time with Skylark's stride. The pretty bay pony was being led by Josie's best friend, Anna Marshall, and as they trotted past the gate, Ellie flashed a beaming smile at Josie.

"Ellie's doing really well, isn't she?"

nother of her friends, Jill
ard her, carrying two cans of
the cans out to Josie.

said gratefully. She pulled the
and took a long drink of icy-
ah, Ellie's doing great. It's hard to
be__ ___ just a month ago she was scared of
horses."

Jill smiled. "Then she met Charity."

Josie glanced over to where her horse, Charity, was looking out over one of the Lonsdale stall doors, her dapple-gray ears pricked. A year ago, Ellie had had a bad fall when she was riding, which had left her with a fear of horses. But then she had moved next door to Josie and met sweet-natured Charity. The gray mare had helped Ellie overcome her fear, and now the little girl had started taking riding lessons again.

Josie felt a rush of love for her horse. "Charity's so quiet and gentle around Ellie," she said to Jill. "It's like she knows Ellie's nervous."

"She certainly didn't look quiet in our lesson today," Jill remarked. "She flew over that last jump."

"She did, didn't she?" Josie agreed, reliving the moment when Charity had soared over the three-foot-high fence.

"If she jumps like that at the show, you're going to do really well," Jill told her. "I bet you win first prize."

Josie felt a rush of excitement. There was going to be a big horse show at Lonsdale in a month, and she was planning to enter Charity in one of the classes. Did she really have a chance of winning the huge, silver trophy?

"Gemini and Tubber are jumping really well, too," Josie said, thinking of the horses that Anna Marshall and her twin brother, Ben, were going to ride in the show.

"Not as well as Charity," Jill said loyally.

Josie was delighted by Jill's words, but she didn't want to seem bigheaded. She tried not to look too pleased. "Well, whatever happens, it's going to be fun," she declared.

"Fun?" Jill echoed, staring at her as if she were crazy. "The jumps in the show are going to be huge. I'm glad that I'm only entering Faith in the Novice class. That's going to be scary enough."

"You'll be fine," Josie told her. "Faith jumped really well today."

Jill looked at the ground. "We didn't jump anywhere near as high as you and Anna and Ben," she said, suddenly sounding uncomfortable.

"But you were riding sidesaddle," Josie pointed out. Jill had had to ride sidesaddle ever since a car accident had left her with an injured hip. "That's much more difficult. I think you're doing amazingly well to be jumping at all."

"Thanks," said Jill, blushing but clearly pleased.

Just then, the lesson in the ring ended. The riders dismounted and, after running up their stirrups, began to lead the horses across the ring.

"Did you see me trot, Josie?" Ellie demanded as Josie opened the gate. "I trotted all the way around the ring!" The little girl's jodhpurs were wrinkled around her ankles and knees, and she was red in the face from the heat. She also had a huge grin on her face.

"I saw," Josie smiled.

"Skylark was really good!" said Ellie, patting the bay gelding. "I want to canter next."

"Fine, but let's wait until it's not so hot," puffed

Anna. She was walking beside Ellie, her face bright red. "I think I'm about to die of heat exhaustion!"

"Here," Josie said, handing the remains of the soda to her.

"Thanks!" Anna panted.

"Can I help wash Skylark down, Anna?" asked Ellie.

Anna nodded. "Sure."

"We'll all help," said Jill.

They headed down to the stable. Josie helped untack the horses, while Jill unwound the hose and turned it on.

The water was cool, and it wasn't long before all four horses had been washed down and were back in the shade of their stalls. Josie took the damp saddle pads over to the fence to dry.

"Thanks, Josie," said Sally, coming over with a saddle on each arm.

"Can I do anything else to help?" Josie offered.

"It's okay. There are no more lessons now until this afternoon," Sally said. "Are you and Jill still planning on coming for another lesson on Thursday with Ben and Anna?"

Josie nodded. "My mom said that she would drive Jill and me over."

"How is your mom's new job going?" Sally asked.

"Very well," Josie said. Her mom had recently started a riding school for physically challenged children at Friendship House, a respite center nearby. "Mom loves being able to teach again."

Josie's mom had used to run her own small riding school—Grace's Stables—using her three horses, Faith, Hope, and Charity. But when the land the riding school was built on had been put up for sale, Mrs. Grace had been forced to shut down. Faith and Hope had found wonderful new homes—Faith with Jill, and Hope at Friendship House. For a while it had looked as if Charity would have to be sold, too, but then the Graces had moved to a house with a field, and Josie's dad had been promoted at work, which meant they had been able to afford to keep the beautiful, gray mare after all. The day Josie learned that Charity could stay with them had been the happiest day of her life.

"I'm really happy the riding school's going well," Sally said.

"Josie! Your mom's here!" Jill called.

Josie looked around and saw her mom's car bumping down the driveway, with the trailer in tow behind.

"I'll see you next week," Sally told her. "Keep up the good work with Charity. She's jumping well at the moment. I can tell you've been practicing hard."

Josie blushed. "Thanks," she said as she waved good-bye to Sally. Then she joined Jill by the stable.

As the two girls led the horses out, Charity and Faith touched noses and snorted. Even though they didn't live together anymore, they were still good friends.

Jill held both horses while Josie put shipping boots on to protect their legs, and then the two friends took them down to the parking lot where Mrs. Grace was waiting. Ellie, who was getting a ride home with them, was standing beside the car.

"I trotted all the way around the ring," Josie heard Ellie telling her mother. "And I'm going to canter soon."

"You're doing great," Mrs. Grace praised her. She looked up at Josie and Jill. "Hi, you two. How was your lesson?"

"Terrific," Josie replied, halting Charity beside her. "Charity and Faith jumped well."

She held Charity back as Jill led Faith up the ramp. Charity nuzzled her arm as she waited.

"My girl," Josie murmured, scratching her horse's silver-gray neck.

The mare lifted her lips to Josie's face.

"She looks like she's kissing you!" said Ellie.

Josie stroked Charity's nose. "She is," she said, smiling.

Jill lived on the opposite side of Littlehaven from Josie and Ellie. As Mrs. Grace stopped the trailer beside Faith's field, Mr. Atterbury came out of the house to greet them.

"Thanks for giving Jill a ride, Mary," he said.

"No problem," Mrs. Grace replied. "It's good for the girls to have some lessons with a full set of jumps, and Sally's a great teacher."

She helped Josie and Jill unload Faith.

"Do you want to go out for a ride tomorrow?" Jill asked Josie.

"Definitely," Josie replied. "How about I come over around ten?"

"Okay," Jill said. "We can go into the woods."

"I wish I could come, too," Ellie said.

"You can have a quick ride on Charity tomorrow before I leave, if you want," Josie offered.

The wistfulness on Ellie's face vanished. "Oh, good!" she exclaimed.

Josie and her mom said good-bye to the Atterburys and got back into the car. "I need to stop at Harker's before we head home," Mrs. Grace announced to the girls. "Charity needs some more oats."

Josie loved Harker's Feed and Tack Store. She could spend ages wandering around looking at the blankets, bandages, and bridles and thinking of all the things she would buy if she had had lots of money.

"It smells nice in here," said Ellie as Josie pushed the doors open and they went into the cool, dark store.

"I know," Josie agreed, breathing in the familiar scent of leather and grain.

Frank Harker, the owner, was standing near the register talking on the phone. He glanced toward them but didn't smile.

Josie was surprised. She'd known Frank since she was little and he was usually very friendly.

"Look, I've got to go now," Mr. Harker said into the phone. "But if there's anything I can do, just let me know. I'll come over this evening, after I've closed the store." He hung up the phone and looked at Mrs. Grace and the girls. "Hello. Sorry about that. What can I get you?"

"Is everything okay, Frank?" Mrs. Grace asked.

Mr. Harker pushed a hand through his graying hair and sighed. "Not really," he admitted. "That was Donna Rudnick on the phone. Her mare's just died of colic, leaving behind a four-week-old foal."

Ellie gasped and Josie stared at him in shock.

"Donna's very worried," Mr. Harker went on. "The foal needs feeding every three hours, and she's never hand-reared a foal before. Her husband, Ray, can't help because he works two hours away." He shook his head. "I don't know what Donna's going to do."

Josie pictured a tiny orphan foal, with a fluffy coat and doe eyes. "Can we help, Mom?" she asked.

Mrs. Grace nodded. "Of course." She looked at Mr. Harker. "Poor Donna. We know the Rudnicks well. Their daughter used to babysit Josie when she was younger."

Josie nodded. She liked the Rudnicks. They were very sweet and they loved horses.

"Josie and I could go over there this afternoon, if you think it would help. We could do a couple of feedings, and I can try to answer some of Donna's questions," Mrs. Grace suggested.

A look of relief crossed Mr. Harker's face. "I'm sure Donna would really appreciate that. Are you sure you don't mind?"

Mrs. Grace shook her head. "Not at all. I've been to the Rudnicks' farm before, so I know the setup."

"Can I come, too?" Ellie asked as Mr. Harker called Mrs. Rudnick. "I love foals."

"I'm sorry, Ellie," Mrs. Grace said gently. "But Mrs. Rudnick is going to be really upset at the moment. It should probably just be Josie and me."

Mr. Harker hung up the phone after a brief conversation. "Donna says she would love some help," he said.

"We'll go over as soon as possible," Mrs. Grace said. "We'll get Charity home and then go right over."

Mrs. Grace bought a bag of oats and then she and the two girls hurried back to the car.

Josie saw the disappointment in Ellie's eyes and had an idea. "You might not be able to come with us this time, Ellie, but you can still help," she said. "Charity will need brushing and feeding before she can go out into the field. If you help me, Mom and I will be able to get to the foal faster."

Ellie's eyes lit up. "Okay."

"That's a good idea," said Mrs. Grace. "In fact, Josie, call Dad on my cell phone right now and let him know what's happening. Ellie can help him with Charity, and we can go straight over to the Rudnicks'."

Josie quickly phoned her dad and arranged everything.

"When will you be home?" he asked, right before they hung up.

"In about five minutes," Josie replied.

"I'll be waiting," her dad promised.

As soon as they got home, Mr. Grace came hurrying out of the front door.

"Ellie's going to help you," Josie explained.

"Great." Mr. Grace smiled at Ellie. "You can tell me what to do, Ellie. It's Josie who normally takes care of Charity." He winked at Josie—she knew he was really as confident looking after Charity as she was.

"Well, first we have to get Charity out of the trailer," said Ellie, jumping out of the car. "And then I'll groom her while you get her feed. I know which brushes to use."

Josie exchanged another smile with her dad.

They unloaded Charity and unhitched the trailer. "Be a good girl for Dad and Ellie," Josie whispered, kissing the horse's soft, pink muzzle. Charity pushed her gently, and, with one last pat, Josie climbed back into the car.

Mrs. Grace started the engine. "Okay," she said to Josie. "Let's go see this foal."

CHAPTER TWO

"Oh, wow!" Josie breathed fifteen minutes later, when she looked over the stall door and caught her first sight of the spindly-legged foal. "She's so gorgeous!"

The foal had a fluffy, midnight-black coat, a delicate face, and a large star on her forehead. Her big, dark eyes were sad, as if she couldn't understand where her mom had gone.

Josie turned to the Rudnicks, who were standing outside the stall next to her. "What's her name?"

"She hasn't got one yet," Mrs. Rudnick replied. She was in her sixties, with short, chestnut hair shot through with gray. Her tanned face was wrinkled, and the lines around her blue eyes were deep with concern. Her husband, a stocky man with gray hair, had an equally anxious look on his face.

"We've just been calling her the foal," he told Josie.

"Frank said she's just four weeks old," said Mrs. Grace with a note of concern.

"That's right," Mrs. Rudnick answered. "Four weeks and two days." She swallowed, a look of anguish crossing her face. "Everything had been going so well. Her birth was straightforward, she'd been feeding well, and now this . . ." She broke off and quickly brushed her hand over her eyes. "I . . . I'm sorry," she muttered.

"Please, don't be," Mrs. Grace said quickly. "It's awful to lose any horse, let alone at a time like this, when you have a new foal to look after."

Mr. Rudnick put his arm around his wife's shoulders. "Sunbeam, the foal's mother, was very special to us. We'd owned her since she was a yearling, and she taught our two children and, recently, our grandchildren to ride. She . . . she would have been twenty next month." He cleared his throat and seemed unable to say any more.

Josie felt sorry for the Rudnicks. It was obvious

that they had loved the foal's mother very much. She tried to imagine how she would feel if Charity died, but it was too dreadful to think about.

"I just don't know what we're going to do now," said Mrs. Rudnick. "The foal needs feeding every three to four hours."

"Well, we're here to help you," Josie told her. "We can feed her and watch over her for the rest of the day."

"That's very kind of you," Mr. Rudnick said gratefully.

Mrs. Rudnick nodded. "Particularly when you must be so busy yourself. Frank told me about your new riding school over at Friendship House."

Mrs. Grace nodded. "I will have to go over there to give some lessons this afternoon," she said. "But I'm sure Josie would love to stay and help while I'm gone."

"Yes, I'll do anything," Josie put in at once.

"We should probably get her next feed ready," said Mr. Rudnick. "It takes a while to cool the milk formula to the right temperature."

Josie watched as Mrs. Rudnick made up a feed by carefully measuring out some powdered milk formula into a clean bucket and adding hot water.

"We are trying to move her away from bottle feedings and get her used to drinking from a bucket. The vet said that since she is four weeks old, the best method for feeding is the bucket. But she isn't picking it up that quickly, which is why she needs feeding more than every six hours—that's the norm for a baby her age." Mrs. Rudnick looked at Josie. "Would you like to try feeding her?" she asked. "Then we can see if she takes to you."

"Okay," Josie said eagerly. "Tell me what I have to do."

"Well, first, you need to dip your fingers in the milk and then try to get her to suck the milk off. Then you have to move your hand nearer and nearer to the bucket until she is drinking the milk herself." Mrs. Rudnick handed the bucket to Josie.

Josie went into the stall. The foal looked up warily, her eyes huge and anxious. "Hey, there," Josie murmured, crouching down.

To her disappointment, the foal retreated to the back of the stall and stared nervously at her.

Josie glanced around, not sure what she should do to make the foal come to her.

"Offer her the milk and just wait until she comes to you," Mrs. Grace urged softly. "It's important to let her make the first move."

Josie dipped her fingers in the bucket and held them out toward the foal. As a few drops dripped onto the straw, the foal's ears pricked. She stretched her muzzle toward Josie, her tiny nostrils blowing in and out as she scented the warm milk.

"That's it," Josie encouraged.

The foal hesitated and then took a step toward Josie. Josie put her hand back into the bucket and then offered it again. The foal was clearly hungry, in spite of her shyness. She moved the last few steps and started to nuzzle at Josie's fingers.

"You're a clever little girl, aren't you?" Josie whispered. Feeling the foal's tongue rasp against her hand, Josie felt a wave of tenderness. The little orphan was so vulnerable and innocent. The filly had no idea of the fight that lay ahead of her.

I'll help you, Josie promised silently. I'll do anything I can.

The foal nudged her hand, and Josie dipped her fingers in the bucket again. Following her hand, the foal bent her head closer and closer to the bucket until her nose was touching the warm milk. Josie slowly moved her hand down until the foal was sucking at the milk. She glanced over her shoulder in delight. "She's drinking!"

"Well done," said Mrs. Rudnick, smiling at her.

Josie wrapped both arms around the bucket, holding it steady while the filly drank.

"It's going to be such hard work keeping her fed," Mrs. Grace said from the stall door. "Are you going to have to get up in the night?"

'Well, hopefully not all through the night," Mrs. Rudnick replied. "The vet said that if she takes to the bucket okay, then we can feed her at midnight, and that should see her through until morning."

"That still doesn't leave you with much sleep," said Mrs. Grace, looking concerned. "Have you thought about finding a foster mare—one whose own foal has died and who has milk available?"

Before the Rudnicks could answer there was the sound of a car driving up.

"That's Dr. Vaughan," said Mr. Rudnick. "He mentioned he'd try and get back to see if she was feeding okay."

"Hello, Mary," Dr. Vaughan said as his feet

crunched over the gravel. "I wasn't expecting to see you here." Josie was instantly comforted by the familiar, deep voice. Dr. Vaughan had looked after the Grace horses for as long as she could remember.

"Frank told us the news and we came right over," Mrs. Grace replied.

"Great," said Dr. Vaughan, looking over the stall door and smiling at Josie. "The more hands, the better. Raising an orphan foal takes a lot of time and attention."

"I was just suggesting that maybe a foster mare could help," Mrs. Grace said.

"It does sound like a good idea," agreed Mr. Rudnick.

"Well, in theory it is," Dr. Vaughan answered. "But in practice, it can be difficult to find a suitable mare. I don't know of any mares in the area who have lost foals recently, and if we can't find one locally, then it will mean the foal's going some distance away, possibly to one of the big farms, which would be very expensive."

Josie saw Mrs. Rudnick's face fall.

"There's also the added problem of this foal's age," Dr. Vaughan went on. "Fostering works best when the foal is a newborn. If there were a suitable mare in the local area I'd say it was worth a try, but a longer journey might be very traumatic for a youngster."

"I really don't want her going a long distance anyway," Mrs. Rudnick said, looking at the tiny foal. "She belongs here."

Dr. Vaughan nodded understandingly. "Well, I'll keep my ears open in case I hear of a mare locally; otherwise, it's going to be a case of hand-rearing her." His expression was somber as he finished talking.

"We'll manage," said Mrs. Rudnick, her voice filled with determination.

Mrs. Grace glanced at her watch. "I've got to get going to the riding school. Will you be okay here, Josie?"

"Sure," Josie said. "I'll be fine!"

Dr. Vaughan and Mrs. Grace left, and, five minutes later, Mr. Rudnick headed off to work, too.

Mrs. Rudnick waited with Josie until the foal lost interest in the milk and wandered away, putting her head down now and then to sniff at the straw.

"The bucket will need scrubbing out before her

next feed," said Mrs. Rudnick. "That will be around three o'clock. Will you be okay giving her that on your own? I need to go and get some work done."

"I'll be fine," Josie said again. She looked at the foal nuzzling at the straw on the other side of the stable. The little horse looked so small and alone. "I'll stay as long as you need me to."

"Thanks, Josie," Mrs. Rudnick said with a weak smile. "Now, why don't we go fix you some lunch, and I'll show you where everything is."

As soon as she had finished her sandwich, Josie made her way back down to the stable. Looking over the wooden stall door, she saw that the foal was lying down, with her gangly legs tucked underneath her fluffy body and her tiny muzzle resting on the straw.

Josie slid back the bolt. The foal lifted her head at once, her body stiffening in alarm.

"It's okay, sweetie," Josie murmured. "You don't need to get up. I'm not going to hurt you."

The foal stared at her, one front leg pushing out as if she were about to stand.

Josie pulled the door shut behind her and

crouched down, waiting. The foal watched her closely.

The minutes ticked by, and gradually the tension left the foal's body. She tucked her front leg back under her body and relaxed. Josie slowly edged over. The foal didn't move. Kneeling down, Josie touched her soft neck.

"Hi, there. I'm Josie. I'm going to help look after you," Josie explained softly. "Your mom might not be here anymore, but there's lots of people who love you and want to help you." She settled down next to the foal and gently scratched her neck. With a contented sigh, the foal let her muzzle rest on the straw again. Josie smiled. She'd been planning on putting some fresh straw down, but she decided that could wait.

"I wonder what the Rudnicks will call you," said Josie. She ran through various names in her head—Star, Beauty—but none of them seemed right.

She needs a special name, Josie thought, looking at the beautiful filly.

Josie still hadn't come up with anything when, twenty minutes later, the foal lifted her head and started getting to her feet.

Josie stood up, too, and stretched. "I'll get you

some fresh water," she said. She took the bucket outside and refilled it. Then she fetched a wheelbarrow, broom, and pitchfork and began to clean out the stall.

The foal watched her curiously, and, as Josie carried a forkful of dirty straw over to the wheelbarrow in the doorway, the baby horse walked over to the broom and began to nibble at it with her teeth. Stepping backward, she pulled the broom with her.

Josie grinned. "Are you trying to help?" She rescued the broom and began to move the pitchfork safely out of the foal's reach as well.

Following Josie to the door, the foal nudged her in the back.

Josie turned and patted her. "You *are* getting more confident," she said, feeling pleased.

The foal hesitated, then butted Josie hard in the chest with her forehead.

"Hey, careful!" Josie gasped. "That hurt!" But it was impossible to be strict with such a cute creature. Josie ruffled the foal's mane. She knew there was a long, hard road ahead for the orphan, but at least the filly seemed to be taking the first steps.

By the time Mrs. Rudnick came back, Josie had put down some fresh straw, swept the aisle, and started to feed the foal again. This time, she had only to offer a couple of handfuls of milk before the filly plunged her head into the bucket and started to drink, her tail swishing from side to side.

"How's she been?" Mrs. Rudnick asked anxiously.

"Fine," Josie replied. "She seems happier."

"That's good," said Mrs. Rudnick, looking relieved. "Thanks for watching her, Josie. I've been so busy." She smiled at Josie. "You are very sweet to stay here. I know this is your summer vacation."

"I like staying here with the foal," Josie said.

"I couldn't possibly take up any more of your time," Mrs. Rudnick replied.

"But I like helping," Josie insisted. She felt she was making great progress with the foal, since she already seemed much less shy and unhappy.

Mrs. Rudnick hesitated. "Well, let's see what your mom says."

"If it makes things easier, Josie's more than welcome to sleep here," Mrs. Rudnick said to Mrs. Grace when the latter arrived a little while later. "The guest room's all made up."

Mrs. Grace looked over questioningly at Josie.

Josie nodded. "That way, I can help in the morning, too," she said, patting the foal.

Just then, the phone rang. "Excuse me for a minute," Mrs. Rudnick said, and she hurried off to answer it.

"Will you feed Charity for me, too, Mom?" Josie asked.

Her mom nodded. "Of course. But tomorrow you'll have to come home and look after her yourself."

Josie felt torn. She knew she had a responsibility to Charity, but the baby horse seemed so needy. "But what will Mrs. Rudnick do? She's really busy."

"I know, but you can't stay here forever," Mrs. Grace pointed out. "You've got Charity to look after, and you said you'd help me with lessons over at the riding school. You can't just forget about those things."

Josie knew her mom was right. "I guess," she said slowly.

"Now, I'll go home and get you some things for a sleepover," Mrs. Grace said.

Josie's mom handed her a cell phone. "Call me at home if you think of anything else. Otherwise, I'll see you in about an hour."

She left, and Josie sat down in the stall. The foal wandered over and lifted her muzzle to Josie's face. "Hi, sweet thing," Josie sighed, stroking her nose. "I'd love to stay here and look after you all the time, but Mom's right. I can't."

The filly nudged her trustingly. Josie felt a little worried. What were the Rudnicks going to do? "I'll stay as long as I can," she told the foal.

As Josie spoke, she remembered Jill. They had been planning to meet up at ten o'clock, but there was no way she was going to be able to make it. She pulled the phone out of her pocket to call Jill.

Jill answered. "Hello?"

"Hi, Jill, it's me," Josie said. After a few minutes of chatting, Josie explained about the foal.

"That's awful!" Jill burst out when she had heard the whole story. "Do you want me to come over and help tomorrow?" Jill offered. "I'm not doing anything."

"Okay!" Josie said. "That'd be great!"

"I could come over whenever you want—it is

summer vacation, after all!" Jill went on. "You should ask Anna and Ben, too. We could take turns helping."

"You mean, sort of like an assembly line?"

"Exactly," replied Jill. "We could visit on alternate days, or something."

'That's a great idea!" Josie exclaimed. "I'll give Anna a call now." She said good-bye to Jill and immediately dialed Anna's number.

Anna was just as enthusiastic as Jill had been. "Of course Ben and I will help," she said, as soon as Josie told her the news.

"That's great, Anna," said Josie, her mind working fast. "If we can cover the day and early evening feedings between us, then the Rudnicks will be able to get their work done in the day and just have the midnight and six A.M. feedings to do." The girls squealed in excitement, agreed to talk in the morning, and said their good-byes.

Pressing the OFF button, Josie jumped to her feet. She was just opening the stall door when she saw Mrs. Rudnick coming across the lawn.

"I had a great idea, Mrs. Rudnick!" she cried.

"Really? What's that?" Mrs. Rudnick asked,

leaning over the door and reaching out to tickle the foal's ears.

Josie explained. "I've been talking to my friends, and they've all offered to come and help feed the foal."

"Well, I'd love the help," said Mrs. Rudnick. She came into the stall and stroked the foal. "We've just got to make sure that you're okay, haven't we, little girl?"

The foal pushed her nose against Mrs. Rudnick's arm. The woman sighed. "I never thought things would end up like this. Ray and I should never have bred Sunbeam. We're too old for breeding horses. Maybe too old for horses altogether." Her face clouded over with sadness. Josie wanted to comfort her but didn't know what to say.

Mrs. Rudnick rubbed her temples and sighed. "Anyway," she said, clearing her throat and attempting to speak cheerfully, "you must be starving, Josie." She went to the door. "I'll go and get dinner started and call you when it's ready. Is vegetable lasagna okay?"

"Yes, great, thank you," Josie replied.

She listened to the sound of Mrs. Rudnick's

footsteps retreating across the lawn, and sank down into the straw.

Josie thought of Charity, Faith, and Hope. She might not have owned Faith and Hope anymore, but she suddenly realized she was very lucky that they were alive and well and living near enough that she could see them whenever she wanted. The Rudnicks had lost Sunbeam forever.

We'll have to help as much as we can, Josie vowed to herself.

Recalling Anna and Jill's offers of support, she thought, not for the first time, how great it was to have such good friends. They had helped her out many times in the past, and now they seemed ready to rally to her aid again.

The foal walked over and blew on Josie's hands. Josie touched the animal's face.

"You're going to be okay," she whispered. "We're going to make sure of it."

CHAPTER THREE

"Josie? Are you up?"

Josie blinked and opened her eyes. Mrs. Rudnick was standing in the stall door. The sky behind her was dark and full of stars.

"How are you doing?" asked Mrs. Rudnick.

"I'm fine." Josie's eyes darted to the foal. The little filly was lying down in the straw, her eyes shut. "What time is it?"

"Ten-thirty," Mrs. Rudnick said. "I can take over now so you can get some rest."

"It's okay, I'll stay longer," said Josie, sitting up.

"No. You go to bed," Mrs. Rudnick told her. "I'll stay with her until the next feeding. After that, she should be fine on her own until morning."

Josie didn't want to go.

"Go on," Mrs. Rudnick insisted. "Otherwise you'll be way too worn out to help tomorrow."

Josie stood up. "I'll be down at six o'clock," she said, stretching her stiff muscles.

"See how you feel," Mrs. Rudnick told her. "Do you need anything else before bed?"

Josie shook her head. "I'll be fine. Good night, Mrs. Rudnick."

"Good night, Josie," Mrs. Rudnick said. "And thank you."

Josie took one last look at the small, sleeping foal and let herself out of the stall. The night air felt cool on her face. She couldn't believe that she'd only been at the Rudnicks' farm since that afternoon. It felt as though she'd been there forever. Before going up to the guest room, she brushed her teeth and changed into her pajamas. Then she set the alarm clock for five-forty in the morning and collapsed into bed, falling asleep quickly.

As soon as the alarm went off the next morning, Josie sprang out of bed. Her thoughts rushed immediately to the foal and how she was doing.

Josie went downstairs and found Mr. Rudnick in the kitchen making coffee. "Morning," he smiled. "Can I get you anything? Milk? Orange juice?"

"Just some orange juice, please," Josie replied. She looked out of the kitchen window toward the stable. She really wanted to go and see how the foal was doing, but she felt she couldn't walk out of the kitchen just yet. She didn't want to seem rude.

Mr. Rudnick followed her gaze and smiled. "Thinking about the foal?"

"Yes," Josie admitted.

"Our daughters were just like that when they were your age—horse crazy," said Mr. Rudnick, handing her a glass of orange juice. "Tell you what, why don't you drink that and then go down to the stable? I'll start making breakfast. Donna's out working on another part of the farm, so maybe you could help me give the foal her next meal."

"Great!" Josie said eagerly. She drained the orange juice in two gulps and hurried out of the house.

The foal was standing in the middle of the stall.

"Hey, little girl," Josie said.

Hearing Josie's voice, the foal lifted her head, her eyes brightening slightly.

Josie went into the stall. "Did you miss me?"

The filly walked over and nuzzled her.

Josie's heart swelled with love, and a smile spread across her face. "I'll take that as a yes," Josie whispered, kissing the foal on the head.

After giving the foal her milk, Josie went inside for her own breakfast. Mrs. Rudnick was pleased to hear that the foal had had most of her meal.

"I think that I might turn her out in the pasture this morning. She and Sunbeam used to go out every day. Will you give me a hand, Josie?"

"Of course," Josie said.

They went outside, and Mrs. Rudnick fetched a small, leather halter from the tack room. "I'm not sure how easy this is going to be," she said. "She's used to the halter, but I haven't gotten around to teaching her to follow properly from a lead rope yet. She always just followed Sunbeam." Mrs. Rudnick buckled up the halter. "There we go. It will be fun to go out in the field, won't it?"

The foal let out a long sigh, as if she didn't care about all the attention she was getting.

Mrs. Rudnick's eyes filled with worry. "I'll try

and encourage her forward while you walk ahead of her," she said to Josie. "Let's see how that works."

Josie opened the stall door. Holding the lead rope in her left hand, Mrs. Rudnick put her right arm around the foal's hindquarters. Encouraging the little filly with her voice, she gently urged her forward.

"Come on," Josie said. The foal hesitated and then walked out of the stall and out of the stable.

Slowly but surely they all made their way to the pasture, the foal following Josie.

Josie opened the gate, and Mrs. Rudnick unclipped the halter. The foal took a few steps and whinnied. Pricking her ears, she looked around as if expecting an answering whinny. When none came, she whinnied again.

Josie was sure the foal was calling for her mom. She glanced over at Mrs. Rudnick.

"I hope she's going to be okay out here on her own," Mrs. Rudnick said.

"I'll stay for a little while and keep an eye on her, if you want," Josie offered.

"Thank you. That would be a huge help," Mrs. Rudnick said gratefully.

Josie settled down to watch the foal while Mrs.

Rudnick went back into the house. The filly paced along the edge of the small pasture, continuing to whinny. Seeing the confusion in her eyes, Josie's heart went out to her. There was no way the young horse could understand what had happened, no way she could know that her mother was never coming back.

Josie stayed with the foal until it was time to leave the field and get the next meal ready. The foal finished half the bucket and had just started to wander away when Josie heard the sound of footsteps. It was her mom and Ellie.

"Hi," she said in surprise. She hadn't expected to see her mom so early in the day.

"Hello," said Mrs. Grace. "Ellie wanted to see the foal, so I thought I'd bring her by. When I called Mrs. Rudnick to see if that would be okay, she told me about your idea for a group effort at foal feeding. It sounds like an excellent plan. I called Anna, Ben, and Jill, and they're coming over so that we can work out who's going to be doing each feeding."

Ellie ran to the gate. "Oh, wow! She's so tiny!" she exclaimed. "What's her name?"

"She hasn't got one yet," said Josie.

"Can I pet her?" asked Ellie.

"Of course," Josie replied. "But don't run or be too noisy—you might scare her."

Ellie climbed the gate and walked over to Josie's side. "Hello, little foalie," she whispered.

The foal snorted and tossed her head.

Ellie laughed and then clapped her hand over her mouth. However, the foal didn't seem to mind. Stepping forward, she butted Ellie with her nose.

Ellie giggled.

"She's looking better," Mrs. Grace commented.

Josie laughed. "She seems to like Ellie!"

"Yes, she does," Mrs. Grace agreed, smiling.

The foal began to nibble at Ellie's T-shirt.

"Stop it, silly," Ellie scolded gently. The foal looked up at her, a piece of material between her lips.

Josie glanced behind her. She saw Anna and Ben walking over with their mother, Lynne Marshall, just behind them.

"Hi!" Anna called out. "Mrs. Rudnick said you were around here."

Seeing all the new people, the foal looked curiously over at them.

"She's so sweet," said Mrs. Marshall.

"Yes, adorable," Mrs. Grace agreed.

"It's going to be really cool looking after a foal," Anna said to Josie. "But I bet it's hard work."

When Jill arrived with her dad, they all trooped into the kitchen to make plans. Mrs. Rudnick got out some milk and cookies. "Please, help yourself," she urged.

Mrs. Grace took a rolled-up sheet of paper out of her bag. "I've typed up a schedule," she told everyone. "What I need you all to do is to put your name down for the mornings or afternoons when you're free to come and look after the foal."

"Can I put my name down?" Ellie asked.

"I'm afraid you're a bit too young, Ellie," Mrs. Grace said matter-of-factly.

Ellie's face fell.

"You can come with me sometime," Josie said, to comfort her.

It took a while for everyone to work out the times when they were going to be free, but at last the schedule was set up.

Anna grinned at everyone sitting around the table. "It's like we're all knights or something, gathered together to carry out an important mission.

I feel like we should be saying a vow. I, Anna Marshall, solemnly promise to help this foal grow up to be strong and healthy."

"You're so weird," said Ben, laughing.

"We should think of a name for the foal," Ellie pointed out.

"Well, if anyone's got any suggestions, let me know," said Mrs. Rudnick. "Ray and I haven't managed to think of anything yet."

The room grew silent as each person tried to think of a name.

"I know," Ellie burst out suddenly. "Let's call her Promise!" She looked around with a broad grin. "It's the perfect name. We're all promising to help her, aren't we?"

Josie tried the name out in her mind. Promise. Yes, she liked it. She looked over at Mrs. Rudnick.

"Promise," Mrs. Rudnick echoed slowly. To Josie's delight, she smiled. "I agree," she declared. "It *is* the perfect name, Ellie." Everyone started clapping, and Ellie smiled. The future was beginning to look much brighter for the foal.

CHAPTER FOUR

The breeze blew against Josie's face as she cantered toward the large fallen tree trunk in the woods by Jill's house. "Easy now," she murmured, her fingers closing on the reins as Charity started to move faster.

Charity steadied herself and took off in front of the tree trunk perfectly. As they landed on the other side, Josie leaned over and patted her neck. "Good girl!" she whispered. She cantered over to where Jill was waiting on Faith. She eased Charity to a halt and the two horses touched noses.

"She jumped that beautifully," said Jill.

"Do you want to try?" Josie asked.

"Maybe just the low end." Jill trotted Faith away. As Jill turned toward the tree trunk, Josie saw a determined look cross her face. Jill urged Faith on, and the patient bay mare cleared the low end of the tree with ease.

"That was great!" Josie called out to her friend.

Jill rode over. "I just hope she's as good at the show."

"I don't know what you're worrying about," Josie told her. "Faith will be a doll. She always is."

Jill smiled. "She is, isn't she? She's just wonderful." As if she knew she was being praised, Faith turned her head and gently nuzzled the toe of Jill's riding boot. "Okay, I'm going to think positively," Jill declared confidently. "The show is going to be fine."

"It'll be more than fine," Josie grinned. "It'll be a blast!"

Josie got back from her ride with Jill feeling tired but happy. After spending so much of the last day worrying about the foal, it had been a relief to be out riding again with nothing serious on her mind.

Walking back to the house, she glanced at her watch. Anna and Ben were probably home by now. Maybe she'd give them a call to see how things had gone with Promise. She went into the hall, picked up the phone, and dialed their number.

Anna answered almost immediately.

"Hi, it's me," said Josie. "How's Promise?"

"She seemed fine," Anna replied. "She drank most of the milk."

Josie felt a huge wave of relief.

"She's just so friendly," Anna continued. "She kept nibbling at our sleeves and pushing us with her little nose. She bumped into Ben so hard he almost fell in the water bucket!" she said, chuckling. "You should have seen his face!"

Josie grinned. "I can imagine! But I think Promise's improvement is worth a few nibbles. You should have seen how miserable she was when I first saw her."

"Are you on the schedule for tomorrow?" Anna asked.

"Uh-huh. In the morning," Josie replied. "I have to help Mom at Friendship House in the afternoon."

"I'll meet you there, if you want," Anna offered. "My mom will be going over to teach an art class."

"Sounds good," Josie said. "See you then."

Josie put the phone down and went to the

kitchen. Her dad was stirring a large pan on the stove while her mom washed a cutting board. Basil, the family's terrier, sat at Mr. Grace's feet.

"Mmm," said Josie, breathing in the warm, spicy smell. "What are you cooking, Dad?"

"Chili con carne," her dad replied. "It should be ready in about an hour."

Josie's stomach rumbled. Her dad was a great cook, and his homemade meals were always delicious. She went over to the sink and picked up a towel to help her mom.

"Anna's going to come and help at the riding school tomorrow," she said.

"Excellent," said Mrs. Grace. "I can always use an extra pair of hands. Did Anna say anything about how Promise is doing?"

"Fine," Josie said, and filled her mom in on what Anna had said about Promise pushing Ben around playfully. "It's great to know she's getting more confident around people, isn't it?" she finished.

"Yes," Mrs. Grace replied slowly, a note of concern in her voice.

"What's wrong?" Josie asked, looking at her mom.

"Well, being confident is one thing, but Promise

also needs to learn to respect people, otherwise it could lead to behavioral problems when she gets older."

"What sort of behavioral problems?" asked Mr. Grace.

"Well, things like pushing, nibbling, head-butting, all of which a foal *may* do, aren't so sweet when the foal becomes a full-grown horse. In fact, it can be dangerous," Josie's mom said.

Josie hadn't thought of it like that. "So, we should stop her from doing those things."

"Exactly, Josie," replied her mom. "Promise needs to learn to trust people, but she also has to respect them. Normally, she'd learn manners from her mother, but since Sunbeam isn't around, she needs us to teach her how to behave. I've got a few books on foals from when Charity was born. It might be a good idea to look through them."

"Where are they?" Josie asked eagerly.

"In the study," Mrs. Grace replied. "I'll dig them out later."

After dinner, Mrs. Grace got the books out, and Josie took them upstairs to her bedroom and settled down to read. She picked up one with a picture of a cute foal on the cover and opened it. There was a whole chapter on hand-rearing foals that explained how raising a foal to be a well-mannered horse was hard, but possible. The handlers should be kind but firm, the book said, and train the foal at an early age.

Fascinated, Josie read on. The book suggested that, as well as learning to wear a halter, foals should be taught to accept having their feet, mouth, ears, and tails touched, and should learn to stand, walk, and trot on the lead and to move sideways, forward, or backward when asked.

Josie's head was spinning. There was a lot for Promise to learn. Maybe Josie could be the one to teach her! She jumped off her bed and went downstairs. Her mom was watching TV in the family room.

"Find anything interesting?" she asked, looking up as Josie entered the room.

"Yes! One of the books is really helpful," Josie said, sitting on the arm of the sofa. "Do you think I could train Promise the way it says?"

"You'll have to ask the Rudnicks," Mrs. Grace answered. "But if they say yes, then I think it's an excellent idea. All the training programs outlined in the books I gave you are very good. Let's talk to Donna and Ray tomorrow and see what they have to say."

"Good morning!" Mrs. Rudnick called out as Josie, Ellie, and Mrs. Grace got out of the car the next day.

"Hi," Josie called back, walking over to the stable. She was longing to ask Mrs. Rudnick whether she could train Promise, but she wasn't quite sure how to begin.

Promise came over to the door as they all approached.

"Hello, girl," Josie murmured. Promise shoved her with her head.

"Hey! Don't do that," Josie said at once, stepping away from the door.

Ellie came over and stroked the foal's nose. Promise nibbled gently at her fingers.

Ellie giggled, but Mrs. Grace, who had walked up behind her, said sternly, "Don't let her do that, Ellie. We don't want to encourage her to start nipping."

Ellie's face fell. Mrs. Rudnick, standing next to Josie's mom, smiled at her. "Mrs. Grace is right, Ellie. Promise does need to learn some manners. We can't let her go around biting people."

Josie saw her opportunity to speak up. "Actually, I was reading a book about foals last night, Mrs. Rudnick," she began, "and it said how important it is to train foals, especially orphans. I was wondering if I could do some training with Promise?"

"That would be a lifesaver, Josie!" Mrs. Rudnick said. "Actually, I've been thinking that Promise needs some basic training, but I wasn't sure I was going to have time for it."

"I could begin this morning," Josie offered eagerly.

Her mom glanced down at her watch. "I could help you get started before I go over to Friendship House."

"Thanks, Mary," Mrs. Rudnick said. "I really do want Promise to grow up to be an obedient and well-mannered horse."

Mrs. Grace nodded understandingly. "A horse friend would help a lot in this type of situation. I could call my friends and see if any of them has a horse or pony that might be suitable."

Just then, one of the farm's delivery vans drove up outside.

"Let me know what you hear. Now, I'd better get to work," Mrs. Rudnick said, and she hurried off.

"Is Promise lonely?" Ellie asked Mrs. Grace.

"Being lonely isn't the problem, Ellie," answered Mrs. Grace. "Foals that grow up on their own often find it difficult to make friends with other horses as they get older."

Josie looked at her mom in surprise. "Really? Why?"

"Because, being alone so much, they don't learn how to communicate properly with other horses," her mom explained. "We need to find a horse that's very patient and gentle, that will teach Promise manners but won't bully her," she finished.

"I hope you find one soon," Ellie said, looking as worried as Josie felt.

"I'll do my best." Mrs. Grace smiled. "Now, why don't you two go and get the foal slip and a brush box and we'll give Promise her first lesson?"

Promise stood quietly while Josie put on the tiny halter, but she snorted and put her ears flat back when Mrs. Grace started to run her hands over her body.

"This is to get her used to the idea of being groomed," Mrs. Grace explained.

Josie watched doubtfully. "She doesn't seem to like it much," she said. "Maybe she's ticklish."

Ellie giggled from the door of the stall. "Like me!"

Josie noticed that Promise looked very tense. When Mrs. Grace touched the swirl of hair on her flank, the foal snapped her head around, her teeth bared. She moved so quickly the lead rope was almost jerked out of Josie's hands.

"Heads up, Mom!" she gasped.

Mrs. Grace jumped backward just in time. Promise shook her head from side to side, making her fluffy mane bounce, and then turned back to Josie as if nothing had happened.

"Bad girl," Mrs. Grace scolded. "No biting!" She reached out and tapped the foal on the nose, but Promise rudely shoved her arm away.

Josie stared at the little horse. This was not a good sign.

"Should we stop, Mom?" she asked quietly.

Mrs. Grace frowned. "Well, I don't want to get

into a battle of wills with her. She has to let us touch her because she trusts us, and that won't happen if we keep yelling. On the other hand, I don't think we should just give up."

"Promise is being naughty, isn't she?" said Ellie. Josie could see that Ellie's blue eyes were open wide as she stood watching from the door of the stall.

"She doesn't mean to be," said Josie's mom.

Josie's heart went out to the midnight-black foal. She reached over to smooth her forelock, but Promise stamped her front hoof, and Josie immediately pulled back her hand. "So what do we do now?" she asked, turning to her mother.

"Let's turn her out for a while," said Mrs. Grace. "We can try again after she's had a chance to run off some of that energy."

Remembering the way Promise had wandered sadly around the field on her own the first time they turned her out, Josie wasn't sure her mom's idea would work. But it was probably better than continuing the training session. When Josie led the foal into the field and unbuckled the halter, Promise butted her muzzle against her hand. *I'm sorry I misbehaved*, she seemed to be saying. *Don't leave me.*

"Oh, Promise," Josie sighed, gently touching the foal's velvet-soft nose with one finger. "I know it's not your fault. I'm sure you'll be great when we start training you for real. We just need to find you a friend, that's all."

"Did you find a horse to stay with Promise yet?" Josie asked her mom as they drove over to Friendship House later that afternoon. They had stayed at the Rudnicks' farm to muck out Promise's stall and sweep the aisle, then dropped Ellie at home.

Mrs. Grace shook her head. "I called a few people, but none of them could help. The only horse I know of that isn't being ridden this summer is a nervous and pretty unfriendly gelding. There's no way he'd work. Promise needs a steady, caring horse to teach her to trust and respect the humans and the other animals around her."

Josie sighed. She knew a horse that fitted the description perfectly. "It's too bad Hope can't go and live at the Rudnicks'. She'd be perfect."

"I know. But I need Hope at the riding school," said Mrs. Grace, turning down the driveway that led to Friendship House. "She's a favorite! All the children want to ride her in their lessons."

Josie nodded. She hadn't really made the suggestion seriously. She knew Friendship House was the perfect home for Hope. The calm gray mare loved having all the children around her, and she was the perfect horse for them to learn on.

Mrs. Marshall's car was already parked outside when Josie and her mother drove up. Anna and Ben's mom ran art classes for the children staying at Friendship House, so it wasn't unusual for her to be there. Josie and Mrs. Grace walked around to the stable at the back of the honey-colored building. Anna was grooming Hope with the help of a boy who looked about seven years old.

"Hi!" Anna called, waving a soft brush. "I got here about twenty minutes ago, so I thought I'd start brushing Hope. Then Tom asked if he could help get her ready for his lesson."

Hope let out a whinny when she saw Mrs. Grace and Josie. With her large, plain head, she wasn't the prettiest horse, but what she lacked in beauty she made up in sweetness.

"Hi, girl," said Josie, walking up and rubbing

Hope's flea-bitten gray neck. Hope nudged gently at Josie's jacket pockets.

Getting out some mints and feeding Hope one, Josie looked over and smiled at the boy. "How are you, Tom?"

"I like grooming Hope," Tom said cheerfully. He walked slowly around Hope and went to the brush box. Josie knew he had lost the lower part of his left leg in a car accident and had recently had a prosthetic foot fitted. When he bent down awkwardly to get a different brush, Josie resisted the urge to help him. She had been around the children at Friendship House long enough to know they liked being able to do things on their own.

As Tom stood up, having retrieved a soft brush, Hope turned her head and nuzzled him. Seeing Tom's face light up, Josie felt a rush of happiness.

Yes, she thought happily, this really is the perfect home for Hope. I could never make her leave.

Later, while Josie's mom gave Tom his lesson on Hope, Josie and Anna groomed Tiptoe and Clown, the two other school horses.

Tiptoe, a pretty, dun mare, whinnied softly as Tom rode Hope past the gate.

"It's great that they all get along so well, isn't it?" Anna said.

"Yeah," Josie agreed. Clown and Tiptoe had just arrived at Friendship House a few weeks before, but it felt as though they had been there forever. Josie sighed. "I just wish we could find a horse like Hope to stay with Promise."

Anna's eyes widened. "I know! We could put a notice up in Frank Harker's store!"

"That's a great idea," said Josie. Mr. Harker would probably be happy to help out, she thought, since he already knew about Promise's situation.

"Let's talk to your mom when she finishes the lesson," Anna urged.

Mrs. Grace agreed with their plan. "But we'll need to check with Mrs. Rudnick," she warned. "If you two can get Clown and Tiptoe tacked up and ready for the next lesson, I'll go and call her now."

By the time Mrs. Grace came back, the three children who were sharing the lesson had arrived and were standing by the horses.

Mrs. Grace smiled at the group. "Hello, everyone. Let's get your helmets on and get you mounted." She turned to Josie. "It's all arranged," she said. "Mrs. Rudnick agreed, so I called Mr. Harker, and he's going to put up an ad this afternoon."

Josie exchanged relieved looks with Anna. Lots of people visited Mr. Harker's store. One of them was bound to have a companion horse for Promise.

The rest of the afternoon flew by. When Josie got home that evening, she was worn out, but she knew she still had to ride Charity. She had a lesson in two days, but, with everything that had been going on, she hadn't had much time to school Charity. And the horse show was coming up. She and Charity needed all the practice they could get.

Charity was waiting by the gate when Josie got to her pasture. She pricked her dapple-gray ears and whinnied as Josie approached.

"Hi, there, girl," Josie murmured, rubbing her warm neck. "I'm sorry I haven't been around that much."

Charity gently rubbed her head against Josie's chest and snorted.

Fifteen minutes later, Josie was riding Charity around the field. The beautiful, gray mare responded eagerly to her lightest touch, and Josie felt her weariness vanish. She was lucky to have a horse like Charity, lively but gentle, spirited but affectionate.

She wondered how different Charity might have been if she hadn't grown up with Hope and Faith. The two horses had looked after Charity, cared for her, loved her, and taught her how to behave. Poor Promise wasn't so lucky.

Maybe Charity could help Promise? Josie thought. But she knew that Charity had never had a foal, and that she might not know what to do. Josie wished that an experienced mare were available to help. She went to sleep that night and dreamed of Promise.

CHAPTER ONE

"Hey, there, cutie!" Josie called the next morning, looking over the stall door after arriving at the Rudnicks' farm. Promise, who had been lying down, scrambled to her feet and blinked a couple of times.

"Does this mean you're in a good mood today?" Josie asked the foal.

Promise blew down her nostrils as if to say yes, and Josie laughed. Just then, she heard Mrs. Rudnick calling her name.

"Josie!" Mrs. Rudnick said again, hurrying toward her. "I just got some great news. A woman named Margaret Henson just called to say she's got two broodmares that could keep Promise company."

Josie's heart leaped. "That's fantastic!"

"I know," said Mrs. Rudnick, her eyes shining. "She saw the ad in Frank's store this morning. Actually, Margaret and I know each other—our daughters went to Pony Club events together—but we'd lost touch over the years. As soon as Frank told her what happened to Sunbeam, she called. Margaret's been looking for someone to look after her horses, because she and her husband want to travel. It seems as if it could be the perfect solution."

Josie hadn't thought there would be an answer to the ad so quickly. "So, when are the horses going to come?" she asked eagerly.

"Margaret's bringing them over later this morning," Mrs. Rudnick answered. "There didn't seem to be any point in waiting. The sooner they get settled in, the better."

"I just hope they get along with Promise," Josie said.

"I'm sure they will," Mrs. Rudnick replied confidently. "Aztec is twenty, and Inca is eighteen. They're very unlikely to bully Promise or hurt her." She looked at Josie with a smile in her eyes.

Josie patted Promise. "Did you hear that?" she said. "You're going to have some new friends."

* * *

For the rest of the morning, Josie thought about the two horses that were coming. What would they be like? How would Promise react when she saw them?

At eleven o'clock, a car came down the driveway pulling a trailer. Josie went over with Mrs. Rudnick to greet it.

"Josie, this is my friend, Margaret Henson," said Mrs. Rudnick as a slim woman with light blond hair got out of the car. "Margaret, Josie's been helping out with Promise."

Mrs. Henson smiled warmly. "Nice to meet you, Josie." She looked around at the farm and the thickly wooded hill that rose up behind it. "Goodness, I'd forgotten how beautiful this place was. I'm sure Aztec and Inca will be happy here."

"Do you want help unloading them?" Mrs. Rudnick asked eagerly.

"That would be great," replied Mrs. Henson. They moved over to the trailer.

Josie lowered the ramp. Inside were two bay horses, both about sixteen hands high—or, roughly, sixty-four inches tall. "The dark bay on the left with three white socks is Aztec," Mrs. Henson explained. "The lighter bay is Inca."

Mrs. Henson untied Inca first, and the mare walked slowly out of the trailer. Josie came forward to stroke her. Inca nuzzled at Josie's hand. "Could you hold her for me while I get Aztec out?" Mrs. Henson asked.

Josie nodded and took the lead rope.

Aztec came out just as quietly as Inca had.

"They're both very gentle," Mrs. Henson said as Aztec looked around, her dark eyes calmly taking in her new surroundings. "Now that they're getting older, all they want to do is graze and stand outside and soak up the sun."

Mrs. Rudnick fondly patted them both at once. "It feels like just yesterday that I was watching them jump in Pony Club competitions."

Mrs. Henson smiled. "They gave Jennifer so much pleasure; they deserve some peace and quiet."

"I really think this could all work out," Mrs. Rudnick said happily. "Should I introduce them to Promise?"

Mrs. Henson and Josie both nodded, and together they led the horses around the house toward the field. Josie had put the filly into the pasture about an hour before, to run off any spare energy she might have had. Hearing the commotion, Promise looked up from where she stood in the middle of the field. For a moment she just stared, and then a shrill whinny burst from her. Josie grinned. She had a feeling Promise was going to enjoy having two horse-friends.

The foal cantered up to the gate and thrust her muzzle through the bars. Very slowly, Aztec reached out her nose. Promise snorted and then, with a toss of her head, wheeled away. She trotted in a circle, her tail high, as if to say, *Look at me!* Coming back to the gate, she bounced to a halt, the tips of her ears almost meeting in excitement.

"Wow," Mrs. Henson commented. "She seems lively."

"I think she's just pleased to see other horses," said Mrs. Rudnick. "Let's bring Aztec and Inca into the field."

As Josie and Mrs. Henson led the older horses into the field, Promise tossed her head and gave a little half rear. The two horses looked at her with mild surprise.

Trotting up to Inca, Promise thrust her head into the mare's side. Inca moved away, but Promise wasn't deterred. She butted her head hard against Inca's flanks.

Inca pinned back her ears and squealed.

"Promise!" Josie said quickly. "Stop it!"

She moved toward the foal to shoo her away. Promise wheeled around and darted back toward Aztec. Nearing the mare, Promise turned away sharply and kicked up her heels in a playful buck.

Aztec shied away in alarm, her eyes opening so wide that the whites showed.

"Maybe she'll settle down if they graze together," Mrs. Rudnick suggested to Mrs. Henson.

But Promise didn't settle down. She trotted around the two horses, trying to feed from Inca and then trying to get her and Aztec to play, just as Promise would have done with her mother.

Aztec retreated to the far corner of the field with her ears flat back. Inca quickly followed her, and they stood by the fence, their bodies tense.

Josie bit her lip. It was heartbreaking to watch Promise try to play with the older horses while becoming increasingly confused by their reluctance to join in on her games. She inched closer to where they stood.

Suddenly, Inca seemed to lose her temper. Pinning back her ears, the old mare squealed and chased the foal away, her teeth barely missing Promise's hindquarters. Promise cantered into the middle of the field and stopped, her dark eyes hurt and confused.

"I'm so sorry. I don't know what on earth is wrong with Inca," said Mrs. Henson, looking embarrassed. "She's normally so gentle."

"It's Promise," Josie said. She hated to admit it, but she knew she couldn't deny the truth. "She's got too much energy, and it's upsetting them. I can understand why Inca's acting that way."

Promise cautiously approached Inca again, but Inca threw her head up in warning, and Promise retreated back to the middle of the field.

Mrs. Rudnick looked disturbed. "This doesn't seem to be working out, does it? I know Promise needs some scolding, but she also needs to be able to play with the horses. That is just as valuable to her training."

"Let's leave them together for a little longer," Mrs. Henson suggested. "Maybe things will improve."

But when a kick from Aztec just missed Promise's back leg a few minutes later, Mrs. Rudnick shook her head. "I'm sorry, Margaret, but I think we should bring Aztec and Inca in. This just isn't working, and I don't want any of them to get hurt."

Josie's heart sank as she watched Mrs. Rudnick and Mrs. Henson go into the field and clip leads on to the older horses' halters. Aztec and Inca walked toward the gate, eager to leave the filly behind.

As Mrs. Rudnick and Mrs. Henson led the older horses out of the field, Promise paced along the fence, whinnying sadly. Josie could tell that the little filly didn't understand why the other horses were being taken away.

"Come on, let's get these two back in the trailer," said Mrs. Rudnick. As Aztec and Inca were led back around the house, Promise began to paw at the ground.

"Easy, girl," Josie said soothingly. But Promise wouldn't be comforted. She began to trot up and down the fence faster, whinnying more frantically.

Josie walked over to her. "Oh, Promise," she said, "it'll be okay. We'll find you somebody."

Trotting over, Promise stuck her head over

the fence and butted it hard against Josie's chest.

It was a gesture of unhappiness and frustration, but Josie knew she couldn't let her get away with that kind of behavior. "No! Promise," she said. "Don't do that!" She reached out to push the foal's head away.

Pinning her ears back, Promise sank her teeth into Josie's arm.

"Ow!" Josie gasped, her hand flying to the tooth marks. Promise's teeth had only just caught her, but still, it hurt. "Promise!" she exclaimed, angry and upset.

Stepping forward and holding her temper, she sharply tapped the little foal's nose as her mom had done the day before. "Bad girl," she said, trying to sound firm but not too angry. "No biting."

Promise looked at her coldly but didn't lash out again. Stamping a hoof, she looked over at the gate and whickered. When no answer came, her head drooped, and she heaved a big sigh.

Josie's heart went out to the tiny foal. The poor baby had had nothing but bad luck. Feeling tears well up in her eyes, Josie wondered if the foal's luck were ever going to change.

CHAPTER ONE

"Your turn, Josie!" Sally called out.

Concentrate, Josie told herself as she rode Charity away from the other horses. It was the following morning, and Josie was in the middle of her lesson. She glanced at the line of jumps down the far side of the ring. There were four in all, each a single pole balanced between two standards. It was a gymnastic—an exercise Sally often used in jumping lessons to make sure that both the horse and rider were balanced and in control.

Anna and Gemini had knocked two jumps down, and Ben had let the horse he was riding, Tubber, run out at the third fence. Sally had put the fences down for Jill, who had cleared all of them.

Josie frowned and tried to force all thoughts out of her head except those of jumping. It was hard. Promise hadn't had any of her lunchtime milk the day before, and Anna, who had taken over on feeding duty after Josie, had told her that the foal had had only a few mouthfuls at her afternoon and evening feeds.

Charity pulled eagerly at the reins, and Josie let her ease into a trot and then moved into a canter.

We can do it, she thought, touching Charity's neck with one hand.

"Keep her straight and your eyes forward," Sally instructed as Josie reached the corner and turned toward the jumps. "Don't give her a chance to refuse."

Josie sat down deep in the saddle. With a swish of her tail, Charity headed toward the first jump in the gymnastic.

Looking straight ahead, Josie urged the dapple-gray pony forward with her legs. They cleared the first three jumps, but then Josie felt Charity begin to hesitate.

Josie squeezed and clicked her tongue, pushing Charity on until they were flying smoothly over the fourth.

"Good riding!" Sally called as Josie patted Charity's neck in delight. "That was very nicely done. Just remember, heels down even when you are pushing her. You can't let your equitation go just because you need to ride her harder."

Josie nodded and cantered over to where Anna, Ben, and Jill were waiting. "That was great!" Ben exclaimed. "You are going to rock at the show."

Trying to hide her proud blush, Josie bent down and straightened her saddle pad.

"Okay," said Sally. "Let's do it again! But this time," she said, grinning, "I think we'll try without stirrups!"

The group groaned and began looping their leathers over their saddles. By the time the lesson came to an end, Josie was sure her legs were going to fall off.

"I ache all over!" Anna complained as they dismounted.

"My legs feel like jelly," Josie groaned. "Twenty minutes without stirrups! That was a nightmare."

"Sally's just cruel," Ben added, unsaddling Tubber.

"Moan, moan, moan," grinned Jill, who had been

excused from riding without stirrups because she rode sidesaddle. She put on a voice like Sally's. "Just think how much it will have improved your balance and your seats and—" She broke off with a squeal as Josie poked her in the ribs with the end of her riding crop.

Stepping backward to escape, Jill tripped over a water bucket. The water splashed up, drenching her. "Oh, no!" she cried, looking down at her soaking-wet jodhpurs.

Josie, Anna, and Ben burst out laughing.

"At least it's a hot day," Jill said, laughing. "They'll dry quickly."

"Yeah, I'm baking," said Anna.

Ben picked up the end of the hose. "I could always help cool you down."

"Don't even think about it!" Anna hastily pulled Gemini out of range of the hose.

"Oh, well, I guess I'd better just wash Tubber down, then," Ben said with a grin. He turned the hose on and began to hose off Tubber's sweaty, chestnut neck.

Josie joined Anna. As they each awaited their turn with the hose, Anna said, "Are you going to see Promise today, Josie?"

Josie shook her head. "It's Jill's turn." She sighed as thoughts of Promise flooded back into her mind. During her lesson she had managed to push those thoughts aside. "I hope Promise is drinking her milk today."

"Me, too," said Anna. "She was so restless yesterday afternoon. I've never seen her like that before."

"What are you two talking about?" Jill asked, leading Faith over.

"Promise," Josie answered.

"I'll call you as soon as I get home tonight and tell you how she is," said Jill. "But don't worry, I bet she's fine."

But when Jill did call, she didn't have good news. "Promise still isn't eating," she told Josie. "Mrs. Rudnick's really worried about her. She's going to call Dr. Vaughan."

Josie heard Jill's mom calling in the background. "I've got to go," Jill said. "But call me if you hear anything."

"I will," Josie promised. "Bye." She slowly replaced the receiver.

At that moment her mom came out of the

kitchen. Seeing Josie's worried face, she frowned. "Are you okay, sweetie?"

"No! It's Promise!" Josie blurted out. Then she repeated what Jill had told her.

"That doesn't sound good," Mrs. Grace said. "Maybe I'll give Mrs. Rudnick a call and see what's happening."

Josie waited anxiously as her mom dialed the Rudnicks' number and listened to her mom's side of the conversation. Mrs. Grace nodded several times and said, "Yes, yes, it sounds very upsetting."

Josie hugged herself with both arms, images of Promise filling her mind. Josie was sure that the foal had stopped feeding because of Inca and Aztec. She knew how unhappy Promise had been after the horses had been taken away, because the foal had bitten her. Josie was convinced she could have saved the little foal from the pain of being rejected. If she'd thought about it more when Mrs. Rudnick had first told her about Inca and Aztec, she might have realized that two older horses would probably not have been suitable companions for a lively filly.

A few minutes later, Mrs. Grace put the phone down.

"What's going on?" Josie asked.

"Mr. Rudnick's away on business and Mrs. Rudnick is exhausted. I think she could really do with some support, so I told her we'd come over. Promise hasn't had a full feed for almost thirty-six hours." She went and picked up her car keys from the hall table. "Come on, I'll tell your dad, and then we can go."

It was a tense drive over to the Rudnicks' farm. The setting sun sent dappled patterns through the branches that stretched above the quiet lanes, but Josie barely noticed the beauty of the evening. All she could think about was Promise.

Mrs. Rudnick met them at the gate. "Thanks for coming," she said. "Dr. Vaughan's on his way, too."

They went to the stable and looked into Promise's stall. The foal was lying down with her muzzle resting on the straw.

"Promise?" Josie said softly. The foal's ears twitched, and she glanced up.

Josie went into the stall. Promise looked smaller than ever in the middle of the straw bed. Josie crouched beside her and stroked her neck.

"She's been lying like this all afternoon," said Mrs. Rudnick.

Mrs. Grace joined Josie. She looked into the foal's mouth and felt her ears. "Have you taken her temperature?"

"Yes, it's normal," Mrs. Rudnick replied. She ran a hand through her hair. "I've tried feeding her, but that didn't work. I don't know what else to do."

Dr. Vaughan's car appeared a short while later. When he saw the foal, he frowned. "When was the last time she ate a full meal?"

"Yesterday morning," Mrs. Rudnick replied.

Dr. Vaughan examined the foal and took her temperature and some blood. "I can't be sure what's wrong until I run some tests. The important thing is to get her eating again as soon as possible. If she hasn't had any milk by tomorrow morning, we're going to have to think about putting her on an IV drip. I think it's important that someone stay with her tonight. I want to offer her fresh, warm milk every hour, to see if that will tempt her to drink."

"I could stay," Josie said, looking at her mom.

"It's fine with me," said Mrs. Grace. "If it's okay with Donna."

"I'd love the help," Mrs. Rudnick said. "Thanks, Josie."

"Call me if you think Promise is getting worse," Dr. Vaughan said. "If I don't hear from you, I'll come back tomorrow morning to see how she's doing."

After Dr. Vaughan had left, Mrs. Grace went back home to pick up some spare clothes for Josie. Returning an hour later, she brought a couple of sandwiches and a surprise visitor.

"Anna!" Josie said in astonishment when the girl walked into the stable.

"I hope you don't mind," Mrs. Grace said to Mrs. Rudnick, who was sitting on an upturned crate beside Josie. "But Anna called just when I got home."

"I don't mind at all," Mrs. Rudnick replied. "It'll be good having the extra help."

"Ben would have come, too," said Anna. "But he's at a friend's for the night. Poor Promise," Anna sighed, looking at the foal. "She will be okay, won't she?"

Mrs. Rudnick and Mrs. Grace exchanged looks.

"I hope so," Mrs. Rudnick said, swallowing. "I really hope so."

* * *

The hours ticked slowly by. Each time Mrs. Rudnick brought out milk, Promise would drink a little, but after a few mouthfuls she'd stop and put her muzzle back on the straw.

Josie, Mrs. Rudnick, and Anna took turns sitting beside her, stroking her and rubbing her ears. They didn't say much.

At eleven-thirty, Josie noticed that Mrs. Rudnick had fallen asleep on the crate by the door. "Mrs. Rudnick!" she whispered.

Mrs. Rudnick's eyes popped open. "Sorry," she said, dragging a hand over her weary face. "It's been a long day."

"Why don't you go to bed?" Josie suggested. "Anna and I can stay with Promise."

"No, I should stay with you," said Mrs. Rudnick.

"We'll come and wake you up if Promise gets any worse," Josie said.

"It would be nice to sleep for a few hours," Mrs. Rudnick admitted. "If I set my alarm clock, I could take over at four o'clock." She stood up and stretched. "Help yourself to anything in the kitchen," she said, as she put the tray down. "And make sure you wake me up if there's any change in Promise."

"We will," Josie told her.

Leaving them alone, Mrs. Rudnick went back to the house.

Anna stroked Promise's neck. "This is awful, isn't it?" she muttered. "I feel so helpless."

"I know," Josie answered. "It reminds me of being with Hope."

"When she had pneumonia?"

Josie nodded. For a while they had thought that Hope might die. But at least they had known what was wrong with her. With Promise, there was no way to tell. It seemed almost as if depression were causing her to fade away, and there was no cure for that.

Anna dipped her hand into the bucket. "Come on, Promise, have some. It will help you get better." But this time Promise completely ignored the milk dripping from Anna's fingers.

Josie's insides tensed with worry. She desperately wanted to help the unhappy foal, but was there anything she could do?

CHAPTER
SEVEN

The hours dragged by. Just before four o'clock, Mrs. Rudnick opened the stall door. "Any change?" she asked.

"No," Josie replied, smoothing the foal's mane with her fingers.

Mrs. Rudnick walked over to Promise and crouched down. "Oh, Promise, why won't you just drink?" she whispered. "Well, you two had better get off to bed, now. Thank you for staying with her."

Josie and Anna looked at each other and stood up.

"We'll see you later," Josie said tentatively.

Mrs. Rudnick forced a smile. "Yes. See you then."

* * *

Josie and Anna fell into bed in the Rudnicks' guest room. Josie was so tired that she thought she would sleep for hours, but thoughts of Promise filled her dreams, and when she woke up, she saw that it was only seven o'clock. She sat up quietly in bed.

Anna's eyes opened almost immediately. "Are you getting up?"

"Yeah," said Josie. "I can't sleep."

"Me, neither," said Anna, sitting up, too. "I just keep thinking about Promise."

"Let's go see her."

They got dressed and went down to the stable. Mrs. Rudnick was sitting by Promise while the foal licked some milk from her fingers.

"How's she doing?" Josie asked at once.

"Well, she drank a little milk," Mrs. Rudnick replied. She tried to smile. "I'm going to call Dr. Vaughan when his office opens and see what he thinks we should do now. Hopefully, we won't need an IV drip."

Josie looked at Mrs. Rudnick's tired face. "Can we get you some coffee or anything, Mrs. Rudnick?"

"Thank you," Mrs. Rudnick said gratefully. "I'd

love some coffee, and, if you don't mind, could you fill the kettle up afterward, so that there'll be some warm water for Promise's next meal?"

"No problem. We'll be right back," Josie replied.

She and Anna set to work. It was good to have something to do, and, after bringing Mrs. Rudnick her coffee and getting the water ready, they put some fresh straw down in the stall and refilled Promise's water bucket.

They were just finishing up when Mrs. Grace called to check in.

Josie filled her in on what had been happening. "Mrs. Rudnick's spoken to the vet. He said that because Promise has had some milk, she might not need to have an IV after all."

"Well, that's good news," said Mrs. Grace. "How much sleep did you and Anna get last night?"

"Not much," Josie admitted. "Maybe about three hours."

"You must be exhausted. I'll come and get you," her mom said.

"Can't we stay until Dr. Vaughan gets here?"

"Sorry, sweetie, but if I don't come now, you're going to have to be there until this afternoon," said her mom. "I've got lessons all morning, and your dad's got to go in to school for a meeting."

"Okay," Josie sighed. "I'll see you when you get here."

Mrs. Grace arrived twenty minutes later.

"Thank you both so much for staying," Mrs. Rudnick said to Josie and Anna as they got into the car. "I'll give you a call later to let you know what the vet says."

"I wish we didn't have to go," said Anna, looking longingly over at the stable.

"It's only for a little bit, girls. I'll bring you both back later this afternoon," Mrs. Grace promised. She looked at Mrs. Rudnick. "You'll be okay today, won't you, Donna?"

"Yes. I'm going to shut the office for the morning, and Ray should be back after lunch," Mrs. Rudnick answered.

Josie watched out of the back window until the farm had disappeared from sight. She really didn't want to leave Promise.

It's only for a few hours, she thought, consoling herself. Just until this afternoon.

Mrs. Grace dropped Anna off at her house and then she and Josie drove home. In the warmth of the car, Josie found herself yawning.

"You look exhausted," her mom said. "Maybe you should go back to bed for a bit when we get home."

Josie shook her head. Although she felt tired, she knew there was no way she would be able to get to sleep. "I think I'm going to take Charity for a ride instead."

"Oh, Josie, I'm not sure that's a good idea. You've only had three hours of sleep."

"I'll rest later," Josie told her. "But there's no way I'll go to sleep now. I can't stop thinking about Promise."

Her mom gave in. "All right, but, take it easy, okay?"

Josie nodded. For once, she didn't feel up to galloping and jumping. A quiet hack would be just fine.

It didn't take Josie long to groom and tack up Charity.

It was a warm day, but the paths under the trees

were cool and Josie let Charity trot on. The gray mare's muscles rippled under her smooth coat and a wave of pride washed over Josie. Charity was in amazing condition. She was fitter than she'd ever been, and, despite everything that had been happening with Promise, Josie didn't think she'd ever been better prepared for a competition. She couldn't wait for the horse show.

They trotted on through the trees. After the tension-filled night, Josie let her thoughts drift as she posted up and down in time to Charity's rhythmic pace.

It was only when she became aware of the reins in her hands becoming slick with sweat that she eased Charity back to a walk.

She glanced around. They'd been trotting for ages. Where were they?

She wasn't on a path she knew well. However, she could hear cars on a road nearby. Josie turned down a path that led in the direction of the sound of traffic. Maybe if she saw the road she would know where she was.

They emerged from the trees a few minutes later. To Josie's relief, the road was familiar. It was the one her mom drove along to get to the Rudnicks' farm. Spotting a signpost, she rode toward it.

She was right. The Rudnicks' farm was just along that road, only five minutes away.

Josie hesitated. Now that she knew where she was, she knew which way she had to go to get home, but, finding herself so close to the Rudnicks', she was tempted to stop by and see how Promise was doing.

Josie quickly made up her mind. She was so close she couldn't possibly go home without stopping by.

I won't stay long, she thought. And Charity could probably use a drink of water.

Clicking her tongue, she touched her legs to Charity's sides and turned down the lane toward the Rudnicks'.

Mrs. Rudnick was just walking out of the house when Josie rode up. She stopped and stared when she saw Charity.

"Hi!" Josie called. "I was riding nearby and thought I'd stop by and see how Promise is doing."

Mrs. Rudnick didn't say anything. She just stood there, looking as if she had seen a ghost.

Josie suddenly felt uncomfortable. "Sorry, I guess I shouldn't have just turned up and—"

Mrs. Rudnick interrupted her. "You know you're always welcome. It's just that your horse looks a lot like Sunbeam. Seeing her took me by surprise. Sorry." Mrs. Rudnick made her way down to the gate. "Can I get you or your horse a drink? She looks quite hot."

"I'd love a drink," Josie said. "And Charity would, too. How's Promise?"

"Well, she's had some more milk," said Mrs. Rudnick. "Almost half a bucket, in fact. It's enough to keep her off the IV."

Josie felt a rush of relief. "That's great!"

"I'm keeping my fingers crossed," Mrs. Rudnick agreed. "Dr. Vaughan called to say the initial blood tests hadn't shown anything. He suggested I put Promise out in the pasture to see if that helps perk her up. He should be by soon." She patted Charity. "Why don't you put Charity in one of the stalls and go see her?"

Josie nodded and brought Charity to one of the empty stalls. Unsaddling her, she fetched a bucket of water, then went to the field to see Promise.

The little foal was standing by the gate, her head hanging down.

"Hey, Promise!" Josie called.

The foal lifted her head slightly and gave a faint whicker. Josie went over to her. "Hello, there," she said. Promise nuzzled her hand halfheartedly.

It was good to see her up on her feet again, even if she did still look utterly miserable. Josie stayed with her for a few minutes before going back into the house. Mrs. Rudnick had put out a plate of cookies and poured Josie a large glass of icy-cold lemonade.

"Thanks," Josie said gratefully.

"I can't believe how much Charity looks like Sunbeam," Mrs. Rudnick said. "Come into the living room. I've got some pictures there. You'll see what I mean."

Josie followed Mrs. Rudnick through the house to the back.

"Look," said Mrs. Rudnick, showing Josie a framed photograph on the mantelpiece. "That's Sunbeam."

Josie stared at the dappled gray horse in the picture. The resemblance between the two horses was startling. Sunbeam looked slightly smaller and stockier than Charity, but they shared the same expressive eyes and fine head.

"That picture was taken about ten years ago," Mrs. Rudnick explained. "Sunbeam had just won an open jumping class at a local show. Do you jump Charity?"

Josie nodded. "We're showing in two weeks at Lonsdale Stables."

She was interrupted by the sound of a low whinny from outside. Josie swung around and gasped. Through the French windows, she could see Charity walking down the path toward the pasture gate.

"Oh, no!" Josie exclaimed. "I should have thought of that. Charity can undo stall doors. I normally put a clip on her door at home, but it didn't occur to me she would escape here. I'll go out and catch her."

Mrs. Rudnick started to leave the room, but then she paused. "Josie, look!"

Josie followed her gaze. On the far side of the fence, Promise had lifted her head and was looking straight at Charity. She pricked her ears and neighed.

Charity whinnied back and, reaching the gate,

stretched out her nose. Promise walked over and pushed her head through the fence. Their muzzles touched.

Josie saw Charity's nostrils quivering as she breathed in and out and then, very gently, nuzzled the filly's neck.

Promise pressed her whole body against the gate, nickering.

"Look at Promise!" Mrs. Rudnick exclaimed. "She's really excited. Maybe it's because Charity looks so much like Sunbeam."

Josie had an idea. "Can I turn Charity out with her?"

Mrs. Rudnick looked worried. "Oh, Josie, I don't know, after what happened with Aztec and Inca. I can't risk Promise being rejected again."

"But Charity won't reject her," Josie said confidently. She looked at Charity, who was still sniffing at the foal. "She'll be fine, I know she will. I know Charity hasn't had a foal, but I really think this will work. Look at them. Promise hasn't looked this happy since Aztec and Inca were here."

Mrs. Rudnick hesitated.

Please say yes, Josie willed her. Please.

"Okay," Mrs. Rudnick said to Josie's delight. "It's worth a try."

Josie opened the gate and rested a hand on Charity's neck. Now that the moment was there to let her into the field, Josie was a little worried. "Be good, Charity," she whispered, aware of Mrs. Rudnick standing anxiously by the fence. "Please!"

Charity blew calmly on her hand. *Trust me*, she seemed to say.

Taking a deep breath, Josie walked through the gate. Promise was standing a little way off, her expression curious but wary.

Josie unclipped the lead and Charity walked into the field. Promise suddenly whinnied and came over to meet her. Reaching down, Charity touched noses with the little foal.

Josie glanced at Mrs. Rudnick. The older woman was gripping the fence so hard that her knuckles had turned white.

There was a moment's pause before, all of a sudden, Promise squealed and wheeled away. She stopped a little way off, her ears pricked, as if inviting Charity to play.

The gray mare trotted after her. They circled once around the field and then Charity stopped.

Halting beside her, Promise butted her muzzle hard against Charity's flank. Josie held her breath. Would Charity teach the little foal some manners?

Quick as a flash, Charity turned and nipped Promise very gently on her neck. The foal jumped and stared at the gray mare with a look of surprise on her tiny face. Charity snorted and trotted away, then stopped and waited for Promise to catch up.

"Would you look at that?" breathed Mrs. Rudnick. "Charity isn't going to let Promise get away with being fresh for a minute!"

Josie's heart swelled with pride. "It's just what she needs," she whispered back.

In the middle of the field, Promise hesitated for a moment, then swished her short fluffy tail and set off at a rapid trot, breaking into a canter after a few strides. Reaching the mare's side, she slowed down and together they walked over to the trough. Charity put her head down and drank as Promise watched. Lifting her dripping muzzle, Charity nudged the foal's neck as if to say, *You have a drink now.*

Promise stepped forward and, standing contentedly side by side, mare and foal drank together.

Josie swallowed. She glanced at Mrs. Rudnick and saw that there were tears in the older woman's eyes.

"I can't believe it," Mrs. Rudnick said again, shaking her head. "Promise looks so happy."

"They both do," Josie agreed in delight.

When Dr. Vaughan arrived, Charity and Promise were still in the field together. Mrs. Rudnick had brought down some milk.

With Charity beside her, Promise had drunk every drop.

"She looks like a different foal from last night," Dr. Vaughan said in surprise. "This is excellent."

"Well, it's all thanks to Charity," Mrs. Rudnick explained. "She's so good with her."

Dr. Vaughan smiled at Josie. "Charity seems to be taking after her own mom, then. Hope was a wonderful mother, wasn't she?"

Josie smiled. "Yes." She sighed happily. "I'm just glad that Promise is drinking again."

Dr. Vaughan nodded. "Foals can go into a decline

very quickly if they stop feeding." He scratched his head. "Of course, the problem we have to face now is what Promise does when you take Charity away."

Josie stared at him. She'd been so delighted about Promise's recovery that she hadn't thought about what would happen when she rode Charity home.

Dr. Vaughan looked at Mrs. Rudnick. "It's clear that a lack of horse companionship is causing some of Promise's problem. You're going to have to find another companion as soon as possible. We don't want her condition to deteriorate again."

"Of course not," Mrs. Rudnick said hastily, and from the shock in her eyes, Josie could tell that she hadn't thought about Charity's leaving, either.

Josie's heart beat fast. The solution to the problem was obvious. She had to leave Charity there. But how could she? She wanted Charity at home with her. And there was the show coming up.

But Promise needs her. The thought thudded through Josie's brain. She looked at the mare and foal, her stomach in knots.

"Can . . . can I call my mom?" Josie asked quietly.

"Of course you can," Mrs. Rudnick said, looking troubled. "But Josie, I don't want you to feel that you have to leave Charity here. I understand completely if you want to take her home tonight."

"I'll just give Mom a call," Josie said. "I'll be right back."

Mrs. Rudnick nodded, and Josie walked up to the house.

Her body felt as though it were functioning on autopilot, but she knew what she had to do. There was no way she could take Charity home, not if it would make Promise ill.

Her mom picked up her cell phone after three rings.

"Hi, Mom, it's me," Josie said. She licked her lips, which felt dry. "I'm at the Rudnicks'."

"The Rudnicks'!" her mom echoed. "What are you doing all the way over there?"

Josie didn't want to go into a long explanation. "I rode over. And you know how Promise has been depressed. Well, Charity's out in the field with her now and they're getting along great! Promise tried to nudge Charity with her head but Charity nipped her, which is exactly what Promise needed, just like you said. And now she's had a whole bucket of milk, and she's looking much better." Her words were getting faster and faster. "I . . . I want to leave Charity here."

"What? You mean overnight?" Mrs. Grace asked uncertainly.

Josie swallowed. "No. I want her to stay until Mrs. Rudnick finds a permanent horse companion. I know that might take a while, but I want Charity to stay until then."

There was a silence. When her mother spoke, her voice was cautious. "Are you sure about this, Josie? You know I'm too busy to take you over to the Rudnicks every day, and it might take Mrs. Rudnick weeks to find the right horse."

"I know," Josie managed to say.

"And what about the show?" her mom went on. "If you're not riding Charity much, she won't stay fit enough to go in a big jumping class, and even if she does, it won't be good for Promise to be left on her own for a whole day."

Josie's heart sank, but she took a deep breath. "I'll just have to miss the show, then. It's more important that Promise is happy and healthy. You should see them, Mom. They're just perfect together. It might be the only chance Promise has. I can't take

Charity away, I just can't." She blinked, tears forming in her eyes.

"Oh, Josie," her mom said softly. "You are very generous. You should be proud of yourself."

Josie knew that if her mom went on like that, she really would start to cry. "So, I can tell Mrs. Rudnick?" she said, suddenly desperate to get off the phone.

"Of course," said her mom. "I'll come over this afternoon with Charity's food, if you're sure this is what you really want to do."

"It is," Josie said.

Charity was going to give Promise a very special gift.

CHAPTER
EIGHT

"You did what?" Anna exclaimed when Josie called her later that afternoon.

"I told the Rudnicks that Charity can stay with them until they find another horse," Josie repeated.

"But you're going to miss Charity so much," Anna said. "It's going to be awful without her."

Josie wished that Anna hadn't had quite such a gift for stating the obvious. "Gee, thanks," she said sarcastically.

Anna was immediately apologetic. "Oh, Josie, I'm sorry. I shouldn't have said that. I think it's an amazing thing to do." Then a thought seemed to strike her. "What about the show? It's only two weeks away."

"I'm going to have to miss it," Josie said.

"But Josie! You've worked so hard. You can't miss it!"

"I'm going to have to. I'm not going to be able to school Charity enough," Josie pointed out. "And I don't want to take her away from Promise for a whole day."

"You could ask Sally if you can use one of the horses from Lonsdale," Anna said. "You could even ride Gemini. I'll ride one of the others."

Josie was touched by Anna's generosity. She knew how hard her friend had been practicing on Gemini. "Thanks, but I'd rather not," she said, sighing. "It's not just competing at the show that's important, it's competing on Charity. I wanted to have the chance to see how well we could do together as a team. Riding another horse just wouldn't be the same."

"I guess so," Anna admitted. "But you'll still come and watch, won't you?" she added anxiously. "It won't be the same if you're not there."

"'Of course, I'll come," Josie said. But she felt her heart sinking. She said good-bye and hung up the phone, feeling strange. It would be weird going to the show but not competing. She wandered over to her bedroom window and looked across the yard at Charity's empty field. Not so long ago, Charity had had to move out of her field, while drainage work was being done, but she'd only been next door at Ellie's house. It was odd knowing that she was a whole car ride away.

Josie felt another wave of sadness creep over her. She knew she'd done the right thing—she just wished she felt happier about it.

The next morning, Josie was cleaning up after breakfast when there was a knock at the door. It was Ellie.

"Where's Charity?" the little girl demanded, almost before Josie could finish opening the door. "Why isn't she in her field?"

"Because she's with Promise," Josie replied.

"Why?" Ellie asked, coming inside.

Josie explained the situation.

"But I'll miss her being in the field," Ellie protested.

"Me, too," Josie said with a sigh. "But Promise needs her."

Ellie thought for a moment. "Then I suppose

we'll just have to get used to Charity being away," she said in a very grown-up voice that made Josie smile.

"If you want, you can come to the Rudnicks' with me, next time I go," she offered.

"Really?" Ellie exclaimed, her eyes lighting up. "Can we go right now?"

"Not now," Josie said, laughing. "I'm helping at Friendship House today," Josie replied. "But I'm scheduled to feed Promise tomorrow morning."

"I'll ask Mom right now if I can come with you," said Ellie over her shoulder as she went to the door. Josie shut it behind Ellie, her sadness lifted for a moment at Ellie's eagerness to help. Maybe things would be okay, after all.

Mrs. Carter said yes, so, the next morning, Mrs. Grace drove both Josie and Ellie over to the Rudnicks'. Charity was sharing Promise's stall and whinnied as soon as she saw Josie's and Ellie's faces appear in the doorway.

"Hey, there," Josie murmured, going over to stroke her. Promise pushed up next to Charity to be petted, too.

"Hello," Mrs. Rudnick called, coming out of the house to greet them. She smiled at Ellie. "Have you come to help this morning?"

Ellie nodded.

"And I thought we might try another training session," said Mrs. Grace.

Josie turned to stare at her mom. "Really? Already?" She hadn't expected them to try again so soon.

Mrs. Grace nodded. "I don't see why not. I have a feeling that Promise is going to be a very quick learner, and, if that's the case, then Charity will have done her a lot of good already. Is that okay with you, Donna?"

"That sounds like a great idea," said Mrs. Rudnick. "Since Charity's been here, Promise has been as happy as when—as when Sunbeam was alive." She blinked a couple of times, then continued. "Charity's lively enough to play with her, but also caring and gentle, like a real mother."

Josie felt the depression that had been weighing on her ever since she had left Charity at the farm lift. She might miss her, but it was wonderful to hear what a good job Charity was doing with Promise.

"Well, I should get back to work," Mrs. Rudnick said. "You'll come and tell me how Promise does, though, won't you, Josie?"

"Definitely," said Josie, a huge smile on her face.

Josie's mom told Ellie to stay outside the stable, just in case Promise acted up again. Josie put Charity on cross ties so she wouldn't get in the way, then buckled the halter on to Promise's tiny head. The foal seemed perfectly happy with the attention, and stood quietly while Mrs. Grace began stroking her ears.

"She's behaving better already!" Josie said delightedly, and her mom smiled.

"Well, let's not jump to any conclusions, but you're right, so far. I think having Charity really has helped."

As if she knew they were talking about her, Charity whickered quietly, and Josie sent a fond glance over to the mare.

Promise tensed a bit when Josie's mom began to stroke her all along her body, but Mrs. Grace kept talking to her in a soothing tone and soon had run her hands all over the foal.

"Good girl," Josie said proudly, keeping hold of the lead rope with one hand and rubbing Promise's forehead with the other.

"I think we can have a turn at picking up her feet next. Would you like to try first, Josie?" her mom asked.

"Yes, please!" said Josie. She was excited to be able to do some real training. She handed her mom the lead and stood close to Promise's shoulder, facing her tail, just as she did when she was going to pick out Charity's hooves.

"All right, Josie. Run your fingers down Promise's left front leg, and then try picking her foot up. But be careful," Mrs. Grace warned. "She might try and pull away. If she does, you must hold on. She has to learn that she won't get anywhere by struggling. As soon as she stands still, praise her, and put her foot down. She'll learn that standing still is more pleasant."

Josie ran her hand down Promise's front leg and lifted her front hoof off the ground. Promise immediately began to struggle. However, knowing what her mom had said, Josie hung on, and, after a few seconds, Promise gave in and stood still. Charity watched closely, as if she wanted to make sure that her new friend were behaving properly.

"Good girl," Josie murmured, lowering Promise's hoof to the floor. "What a very good girl."

"That was excellent," Mrs. Grace said. "She is a quick learner—just as I thought. Now, wait a few minutes, and then try again. When she's completely comfortable with this hoof, you can move on to the others."

While Josie waited, she rubbed Promise down. It was weird to think that her mom had followed the same training program with Charity so many years before.

I would have been even younger than Ellie, Josie thought, glancing at Ellie watching by the stable door.

Josie tried picking up Promise's hoof again. The filly hesitated and then willingly raised her foot. Soon Promise was standing quietly while Josie picked up whichever hoof she wanted.

"She's doing well," Mrs. Grace said, looking pleased. "I think we should give her a break. It's important to keep any training session short so she doesn't get bored." She glanced at her watch. "I have to get to Friendship House, but you can repeat the lesson in a little while. Make sure you cross-tie Charity first, though."

Josie went over and unclipped Charity and led her into the stall. "It's amazing how big a difference Charity's made to Promise in just one day," she said.

Her mom nodded. "It just goes to show how important it is for foals to be socialized with other horses as well as with people."

Promise raised her nose to Ellie's face and blew softly down her nostrils. "Promise!" Ellie giggled. "That tickles!"

"That's her way of making friends," Josie said. "If you blow back gently, she'll know you want to be friends, too."

Ellie breathed into Promise's nostrils. Promise drew in a deep breath and then blew out.

A huge smile appeared on Ellie's face. She stroked Promise's neck. The foal gently rubbed her forehead against Ellie's chest.

"Are we friends now?" Ellie asked, glancing quickly at Josie.

Josie smiled, feeling a warm glow of happiness. "Yes, you're friends."

Ellie's eyes lit up, and she touched Promise's face. "I'll always be your friend, Promise," she whispered.

Over the next two weeks, Promise continued to make rapid progress. Although Josie couldn't work with her every day, the little foal never seemed to forget anything, and soon she was leading perfectly at both a walk and a trot. And her manners were much, much better, thanks to Charity's keeping her in line. Josie couldn't believe that this was the same filly that had bitten her arm.

The satisfaction that Josie got from training Promise almost made her forget about the show. Almost, but not quite.

"You're still going to come and help us set up for the show tomorrow, aren't you?" Anna said, when she called two days before the big event.

"Of course I am," Josie said, trying to sound as if she were looking forward to it.

"Great," Anna enthused. "There's a lot to get done. We've got to put all the jumps out and clean the barn; then we have to bathe the horses and clean the tack. It'll be fun."

"Yeah," Josie forced herself to say. "Lots of fun."

Putting down the phone, she took a deep breath. She didn't want to go to Lonsdale Stables the next day. She didn't want to have to help get everything ready for the show knowing that she wasn't going to be able to take Charity. But if she didn't go, Anna, Ben, and Jill would worry that she was mad at them. And she didn't want that.

Josie squared her shoulders.

It'll be fine, she thought. Just fine.

Josie arrived at Lonsdale Stables the following morning wearing a cheerful smile. But, as the morning wore on, her determination began to fade. It was hard to set up the course knowing that she wasn't going to have a chance to jump it, to listen to everyone talking about their classes knowing that she wouldn't be joining in.

"Just look at all these jumps," Anna said happily, gazing around at the fences they had dragged into place for the over-fences classes. "I can't wait till tomorrow."

Josie looked around the course and felt a stab of jealousy. She would have given almost anything to be able to take Charity to the show the next day. To hide her feelings, she picked up a pole and started dragging it over to the last fence.

Ben joined her and picked up the other end. "Are you okay, Josie?" he asked in a low voice.

"Me?" Josie said, startled. "Yeah, yeah, I'm fine."

Ben frowned, his brown eyes filled with sympathy. Unlike his extroverted twin sister, he was very good at reading people's feelings. "Are you sure? You've been kind of quiet this morning."

"I'm fine," Josie insisted, forcing herself to smile. She quickly tried to distract him. "So, are you looking forward to jumping tomorrow, too?"

"Definitely," he said, his face lighting up. "Tubber's been doing great in our lessons." He looked at her. "You must really wish you could bring Charity."

Josie hesitated. She didn't want to be a downer, but she knew Ben would understand. "Yes," she sighed. "I'd love to bring her. Not just for the jumping but for everything. You know, getting her ready, waiting for the classes to start, talking about it afterward."

"I know what you mean." Ben frowned. "But

couldn't you enter her? Even if she's not fit enough to jump, you could take her in a flat class or something."

"I can't," Josie answered. "It wouldn't be fair to leave Promise on her own for the day."

Ben looked thoughtful. "But, what about . . ."

Before he could finish, Anna came over. "You two look serious," she said. "What are you talking about?"

"Nothing," Josie replied quickly. She hoped Ben wouldn't say anything. She knew Anna would hate to hear that she was feeling unhappy.

"Well, come on, then," Anna said. "Sally wants us to finish putting up the course."

Josie and Ben exchanged looks. "Coming," they said in unison.

The rest of the day passed by in a blur of activity. After setting up the course, the friends swept and washed down the aisles of the barn, and then it was time to start on the horses.

Josie volunteered to groom. As she brushed horse after horse, people bustled all around her, carrying buckets of water, shampoo, and saddle soap and talking about the show.

It was strange working in the midst of all the activity, yet not really being part of the show. It didn't help that every so often, Josie would catch Ben, Anna, and Jill in animated conversations that they broke off abruptly whenever she approached.

Josie was sure they were trying to be nice by not talking about the show in front of her, but watching them spring guiltily apart made her feel more left out than ever.

At three o'clock, Jill left to get Faith ready, and Ben set off on his bike for the stable at Littlehaven, where Tubber was kept. Josie helped Anna clean Gemini's tack. Then, to her relief, her dad came to pick her up.

"I've got to go," she told Anna, chucking her sponge in a nearby bucket of water.

"Okay, see you tomorrow," Anna replied. "You will be here to cheer for us all, right?"

Josie felt a flash of annoyance. Okay, sensitivity was never going to be Anna's strong point, but couldn't her best friend be a little more understanding about how hard it was to be missing out on the show? "Yes, I'll be here," she said.

She half hoped that Anna would hear the

irritation in her voice, but Anna seemed oblivious. She just smiled and waved good-bye.

Josie stormed over to the car.

"Did you have fun?" her dad asked as she opened the door and got in.

"Yeah, tons," Josie muttered sarcastically. But when she saw the surprise on his face, she felt bad for taking her frustration out on him. "Sorry, Dad. It actually hasn't been that great a day. Can we stop by the Rudnicks' on the way home? I'd like to check on Charity and Promise." She knew that seeing the two horses would make her stop feeling sorry for herself.

Her dad hesitated. "Sorry, sweetie," he said, looking awkward. "I . . . um . . . I've got stuff to do back at the house."

"Oh." Josie frowned. "Do you think Mom will take me when she gets home from Friendship House?"

"I doubt it. She called to say she's going to be out running errands," said Mr. Grace.

Josie sank gloomily back into the seat, feeling as if the whole world were against her.

When she got home, she found it hard to concentrate. She tried reading a book and then looking through a magazine, but she just couldn't seem to focus on anything. After wandering aimlessly through the house, she called Jill.

"I'm sorry, she's not here right now, Josie," Mrs. Atterbury told her. "I can have her give you a call when she gets in."

"Okay, thanks," Josie said with a sigh. She put the phone down and wondered who else she could call. Anna would still be at Lonsdale and Ben would be with Tubber. Feeling extremely lonely, she went out to the yard.

Basil bounded up to her and dropped a ball hopefully at her feet. Josie ruffled the wiry, brown-and-white fur on his head and then, picking up the ball, chucked it across the yard. Basil raced after it in delight.

"Come on, boy," Josie said as he bounded back with the ball. "Let's go to the field. You can run some more there."

She took him into the field and began to throw the ball as far as she could. Basil charged around, yapping loudly, his stubby tail wagging quickly in delight.

"He certainly seems to be enjoying himself!"

Josie glanced up and saw Mrs. Carter looking over the fence. The Carters' yard bordered Charity's field, which was one of the reasons that Ellie was always around. Mrs. Carter had pruning gloves on and a pair of shears in her hand.

Josie smiled as Basil came hurtling back to her with the ball in his mouth. "He doesn't normally get to play in the field when Charity's here."

Mrs. Carter nodded understandingly. "Ellie's really been missing Charity," she said. "I do appreciate your letting her help out so much, Josie. I hope she hasn't been a nuisance."

"Not at all," Josie said. "She knows a lot and it's been really helpful having her around when I'm training Promise."

"She just adores that foal," Mrs. Carter said. "In fact . . ." She broke off. "It doesn't matter," she said, as if she had changed her mind about what she was going to say. "Well, I'd better get going. I'll see you tomorrow at the show."

Josie nodded. "See you then."

As Mrs. Carter walked away, Basil dumped the ball at Josie's feet again. Josie sighed and picked it up. Once again, except for Basil, she was alone.

By the time Josie went to bed that night, she was feeling unusually depressed. Jill hadn't called her back, and when she had called Anna, all Anna had wanted to do was talk about the show.

I'll go and see Charity and Promise before the show, Josie thought as she turned off her light. That'll make me feel better.

When she woke up the next morning, the sun was shining through an opening in the curtains. Getting up, Josie looked out the window. The sky was a crystal-clear, pale blue. It looked as though it were going to be a beautiful day for the show.

Typical, Josie found herself thinking, but she quickly squashed the thought. I am not going to be in a bad mood, she told herself determinedly. I'm going to go over and see Charity and Promise, and then I'm going to go to the show, and I'm going to enjoy the whole thing.

She got dressed and went downstairs. Her mom was making French toast in the kitchen. "Do you want a ride to the Rudnicks' farm first thing?" her mom asked.

"Yes, please," Josie replied.

Mrs. Grace glanced at her watch. "Well, let's try and leave sooner rather than later."

"It's only seven-thirty," Josie said in surprise.

"I know," said Mrs. Grace. "But if you want to get to the show in time for the jumping classes, then we should probably get an early start."

Josie shrugged. "Okay."

She barely had time to eat a piece of toast before her mom was heading for the door, car keys in hand. "Come on, then, let's go."

Putting her plate in the sink, Josie joined her mom at the door. Her dad was coming downstairs, too, dressed and ready to go out. "Where are you going?" Josie asked.

"I thought I'd come with you and then check out the show," said Mr. Grace.

Josie stared at him. "Why?"

"Well, it's such a beautiful day," Mr. Grace replied. "And I haven't seen Charity for a while." He opened the door and started to walk outside. "What are we waiting for? Come on."

Slightly bewildered, Josie followed him and her mom outside.

She saw her parents exchange a quick smile as

they drove up to the Rudnicks' farm. Wondering why they were behaving so strangely, Josie got out of the car. When she reached the gates, she stopped dead in her tracks.

Charity was standing in the yard wearing a brand-new, black-and-white show rug, with her mane neatly braided. Promise stood next to her. The little foal was wearing a new leather halter, and her black mane and tail were washed to fluffy perfection.

"Hello, Josie!" Mrs. Rudnick called, coming out of the house with Mr. Rudnick. They were both smiling broadly.

Josie couldn't believe her eyes.

CHAPTER ONE

"What . . . what's going on?" Josie stammered.

"Charity's going to the show," announced her mother, her eyes twinkling.

"But, how?" Josie said in astonishment. "She's not in shape, and what about Promise?"

"Promise is going, too," said Mr. Grace. "You're going to enter them in the mare-and-foal show class."

"What?" Josie gasped.

"It was your friend Anna's idea," Mrs. Rudnick explained. "Ben, Anna, and Jill called yesterday and asked if you could enter Charity and Promise in the mare-and-foal class." She smiled. "I thought it was a great idea, so I called your mom and we arranged it."

"We all came here last night and got Charity and

Promise ready," Mrs. Grace said. "Even Ellie helped."

"So, is that why no one was around yesterday evening?" Josie asked.

"Exactly," Mrs. Grace smiled.

Josie smiled as she thought about her friends. She should have known that Anna could not really have been that insensitive. Her best friend had come through for her—and for Charity.

"You do want to go to the show, don't you, Josie?" Mrs. Rudnick asked anxiously. "I mean, I know it won't be the same as entering the jumping classes. . . ."

"Charity and Promise can participate in the mare-and-foal class, but they won't be able to actually compete for a ribbon," Mrs. Grace said. "You see, it's a show class for mares that have actually given birth to foals."

"I don't care," Josie said, excitement starting to filter through her shock. "It will be great." She imagined leading Charity and Promise around a show ring with everyone watching. They both looked beautiful. It would be great to have a chance to show them off, even if she couldn't win a ribbon.

Then, she pointed something else out. "Charity's wearing a new blanket."

"The Rudnicks bought it for her," said her dad.

"We're so grateful for everything you and Charity have done for Promise," Mr. Rudnick explained. "We hope you'll see the blanket and the entry into the show as our way of saying thank you."

Josie gulped. "Wow . . . thanks."

"It's our pleasure," Mrs. Rudnick said warmly. "And I really mean that. It's been a lot of fun getting Charity and Promise ready for the show. I've been so caught up with worrying about Promise recently that I'd forgotten how much fun you can have with horses."

Mr. Rudnick nodded. "Me, too. It's been great."

Seeing their smiling faces, Josie had the sudden feeling that Charity's stay at the farm hadn't just helped Promise but had helped the Rudnicks, too. They certainly didn't look as if they thought they were too old for horses anymore.

A few minutes later, as Mr. Rudnick drove the trailer over, Josie started to feel anxious. "What if Promise doesn't want to go into the trailer?" she asked her mom.

"Don't worry," Mrs. Grace reassured her. "I practiced with her yesterday and she loaded just fine. In fact," she added, "I was very impressed with how obedient she's become. You must have been working very hard with her, sweetie."

Josie blushed.

"It isn't easy to train a foal. You should be very proud of yourself," her mom added.

Josie had loved every minute of training Promise, and her mom's praise meant a lot to her. "I couldn't have done it without Charity," she said.

While Mr. Rudnick parked the trailer, Mrs. Grace led Charity inside. Josie followed with Promise. The little foal walked confidently up the ramp, stopping happily beside Charity.

"Good girl," Josie said, patting Promise, who nuzzled her with tiny, velvety lips. The Rudnicks put the ramp up, and Josie climbed out the side door.

"Okay, then," said Mr. Rudnick. "Let's go!"

Lonsdale Stables was busier than Josie had ever seen it. Sally had roped off one of the fields for people who weren't from the riding school to park their trailers in. As Josie's dad drove across the grass behind the Rudnicks' trailer, Josie looked around. There were horses and ponies everywhere, being groomed or warmed up or waiting by the show ring.

"Promise is probably going to be very excited," Mrs. Grace warned as they got out of the car. "After all, it's the first time she's seen this many horses. And Charity hasn't been to a show for a while, so I think it might be best to walk them both around and let them have a good look at everything."

"All right," Josie agreed.

While her dad went to get the number she would need for the show ring, she, her mom, and the Rudnicks unloaded Charity and Promise.

Once out of the trailer, Promise stared around at the showground, her eyes almost popping out of her head. "It's okay," Josie said soothingly, as Mrs. Grace held Charity and the Rudnicks put the ramp back up.

Promise wheeled around in excitement and pulled so hard on the lead she almost dragged Josie off her feet.

"Do you want me to take her?" Mrs. Grace offered. But before Josie could reply, Charity whickered softly and nuzzled the foal.

As the mare's and foal's muzzles met, Josie saw

Promise relax. *It's all right,* Charity seemed to say, *I'm right here.*

Promise snorted, her eyes growing calmer.

Josie rubbed Charity's neck. "You know, you may not be Promise's real mother, but you're as good a mom as any mare could be."

"She certainly is," Mrs. Grace agreed. "You know, I never really thought she was that maternal, but, since she's been with Promise, I've begun to change my mind."

Just then, the Rudnicks came over. "What can we do to help?" Mr. Rudnick asked.

"I think we're pretty much all set," said Mrs. Grace. "Josie and I are just going to walk these two around for a while."

"In that case, I think we'll go and have a look around," Mrs. Rudnick said.

Mr. Rudnick nodded. He looked almost as excited as Josie felt. "It's really good to be at a horse show again," he declared, his eyes twinkling.

Josie and her mom began to lead Charity and Promise around the showground.

"How will it work in the ring, Mom?" Josie asked. "Will I have to lead both of them, or are you coming into the ring, too?"

"Actually, Ellie's going to help you. She asked last night if she could lead Promise, and I said yes," Mrs. Grace replied. "I'll be by the ring in case there's any problem, but I'm sure Promise will be fine up there near Charity." She glanced at her watch. "Ellie should be here soon. Her mom said she'd bring her by nine-thirty."

Mrs. Grace was right.

Ten minutes later, Ellie came running across the showground toward them. She was wearing a new riding jacket, jodhpurs, and boots that were polished to a mirrorlike shine.

"Hi, Josie!" she said, her curls bouncing on her shoulders. "What did you think of your surprise?"

"It's great," Josie smiled. "Thanks for helping get Promise and Charity ready."

Ellie beamed back at her. "It was fun. And your mom said I could take Promise in the ring with you."

Mrs. Carter joined them. "Hello, Mary. Hello, Josie," she said. "You don't mind Ellie leading Promise in the ring, do you, Josie?"

"Of course not," Josie said.

"Have you seen Jill yet?" Ellie asked. "She won

first place in her flat class with Faith. Even though there were no jumps, she's really happy!"

"Oh, wow!" Josie said. "Where is she?"

"She's over by the jumping ring," Mrs. Carter told her. "I think she's about to go in her next class."

"Can we go and watch?" Josie asked her mom.

Mrs. Grace nodded. "Charity and Promise seem to have settled down nicely. Let's take them over there."

They headed toward the jumping ring.

"There's Jill!" said Josie, pointing to the warmup area. Jill was sitting calmly on Faith. The bay horse's coat was shining like a new penny, and her socks and blaze were a perfect, snowy, white. Jill looked great, too. She was wearing a sidesaddle skirt over navy jodhpurs. A frown creased her face as she watched a horse and rider going around the course.

"Jill!" Josie called.

Jill turned. "Hi!" she cried, her eyes lighting up. She began to ride over. "Josie, what did—"

She was interrupted by a shriek. "Josie! You're here!"

Josie swung around and saw Anna trotting toward her on Gemini. She was closely followed by Ben, on Tubber.

"Hi," Josie smiled as they all halted in front of her.

"So?" Ben prompted, his eyes scanning her face.

"What do you think?" Anna asked.

"You are happy, aren't you?" Jill asked anxiously.

"Yes, I'm happy," Josie said with a grin. She looked around at her friends. It was amazing to think they had all gone to such effort just for her. "It was the best surprise ever!"

"I knew you'd be happy," Anna declared.

"It was Anna's idea," Jill said.

"But everyone helped," Anna added.

"Don't Promise and Charity look absolutely beautiful?" asked Jill.

"Just perfect," Josie agreed, stroking Charity's gleaming neck. "But, then, so do Faith, Gemini, and Tubber," she said, looking admiringly at the other horses. "Ellie said you won your flat class," she said to Jill.

Jill blushed and nodded.

"That's fantastic! Congratulations!" Josie exclaimed.

Suddenly, the loudspeaker crackled. "That was Emma Mitchell, on Skylark. Next in the ring is the last competitor in this class, number sixty-four—Jill Atterbury, riding her horse, Faith."

"Jill, that's you!" Anna cried.

"Oh, my gosh!" Jill suddenly looked panicked. "I don't think I can do this."

"Yes, you can," Josie told her. "You know the course, don't you?"

Jill nodded.

"Well, just go in and jump the jumps," Josie said.

"You'll be fine," Mrs. Grace agreed. "You know Faith can jump those heights easily."

Jill took a big, deep breath. "Stay calm," she murmured to herself. She patted Faith's neck. "Come on, girl. We can do it."

"Good luck," someone called as she rode toward the ring.

Jill and Faith picked up a canter and started toward the first jump. Watching Faith approach the first fence, Josie held her breath.

Please let them get around okay, she prayed.

She didn't have to worry. Faith jumped steadily, and they finished with a clear round. Jill rode out beaming.

"Faith was so good!" she gasped.

"So were you," Josie told her.

"Now, you've just got a jump-off to go," said Ben.

"There's only five clear rounds, which means you'll definitely get a ribbon."

"You'll have to go pretty fast," Anna added.

"Yes, really try to push her forward," said Josie, knowing that the fastest horse with the least faults in the jump-off would win the class.

But Jill shook her head. "No. I'm just happy that Faith jumped clear. She doesn't like jumping really quickly. I'm just going to try and get a clear round again."

"That's very sensible," said Mrs. Grace. "Faith isn't the fastest horse in the class, but she could still do well if she gets another clear round. People often make mistakes when they try to jump too fast."

Mrs. Grace was right. Although the first two horses to go went clear with fast times, the other two horses both knocked jumps down. When it was Faith's turn, Jill took the course at a careful pace and jumped another clear round.

"She's third!" Anna cried, hugging Josie.

Josie, Ben, Anna, and Mrs. Grace clapped and cheered as Jill rode out of the ring. Jill hardly had time to accept their congratulations before she was being called back into the ring to collect her ribbon.

"Come on, Anna. We should get warmed up," said Ben. "Our class is next."

Anna nodded. "You're going to watch us, aren't you?" she asked Josie. "We both ride near the beginning."

"I'll watch," Josie promised.

"And, now, for a victory lap," the announcer called to the riders in the ring.

There was a burst of music and the winners in Jill's class cantered around the ring in winning order.

Josie's heart swelled with pride as she watched steady, patient Faith cantering around the ring in third place. It was hard to imagine that not so long ago, Jill had been frightened of jumping sidesaddle. Faith had certainly changed that.

Josie turned to see her mom's eyes shining happily.

As their gazes met, Mrs. Grace smiled. "I guess this shows that things do work out for the best," she said softly.

Josie nodded. She guessed her mom was thinking about having to sell Faith. It had been awful, but, if they hadn't, Faith and Jill wouldn't have been as happy now as they were.

"Yes," she said, smiling, too. "I guess they do."

It was fun watching Ann and Ben. Josie thought she would feel envious, but, standing by Promise and Charity, she didn't feel jealous at all. There would be other shows, with other jumping classes, in the future, but she only had one chance to show Charity and Promise in a class together.

Ben and Tubber jumped a smooth, clear round, making even the difficult jumps look easy.

Josie cheered loudly as Ben cantered out of the ring. "It's Anna next," she said to her mom.

Anna's round was faster, but less consistent. A few times she got too close to the jump, making the takeoff seem jerky and uncomfortable for herself and her horse.

However, she got around clear, too, and rode out grinning broadly.

"Way to go, Anna!" Josie cried as Anna trotted up, patting Gemini's bay neck over and over again.

"He was amazing! We're going to win that trophy!" Anna declared. "I just know we are!"

But although Gemini jumped another clear round in the jump-off, Ben and Tubber managed to jump the course two seconds faster than Anna had.

"Ben's in the lead!" Josie gasped, as Ben crossed the finish line. They all clapped madly, and Ben rode out looking stunned.

"You beat me," said Anna, looking almost disappointed as he rode over. But then her face split into a grin. "Well done!" she said generously. "That was a fantastic round, Ben."

"Thanks," Ben stammered, still looking shocked. "I can't believe we're in the lead."

"Well, you are," Josie said. "And I think you're going to win."

She was right. No one else in the jump-off beat Tubber's time, and, after the last horse had finished, Ben rode into the ring to collect the first-place ribbon and trophy. Even though it was exactly what Josie had hoped to win riding Charity, she realized she couldn't have felt more pleased.

"This is turning into an amazing day," Jill said happily as the two girls watched Anna receive her ribbon for second place.

Josie grinned, starting to feel butterflies in her stomach. "I hope we're still saying that after the mare-and-foal class!"

CHAPTER
TEN

By the time the mare-and-foal class started, a large crowd had gathered. It was a popular class for spectators to watch, and, as Josie and Ellie led Charity and Promise toward the entrance, people pointed at the black filly, who was by far the smallest foal there.

"Oh, look at that one."

"Isn't she cute?"

"She's so tiny!"

As if Promise knew she was the center of attention, she arched her neck and swished her fluffy tail. Holding tightly on to the lead rope, Ellie looked proud enough to burst.

Josie knew just how she felt. Charity walked

beside Josie with a swinging stride, her dark eyes lively and inquisitive, the dapples on her silvery coat gleaming.

My Charity, Josie thought proudly. My beautiful, sweet girl.

They passed the corner of the ring where all their supporters were gathered—Mr. and Mrs. Grace, Mr. and Mrs. Rudnick, the Atterburys, Mrs. Carter, Mrs. Marshall, and the twins.

Josie caught her mom's and dad's eyes. They were smiling proudly. She smiled back.

The judge made the competitors walk around the ring several times. Then, they had to line up to be inspected. The judge worked his way down the line, looking at each mare in turn before asking all of their handlers to trot them out in a straight line.

Several of the foals were quite frisky. The first two bucked and tried to pull away from their handlers, and the third foal, a handsome bay colt who was in line next to Promise, kept squealing and nipping at his handler.

"I hope Promise doesn't do that," Ellie whispered to Josie.

Josie felt slightly worried. If she'd known about

the show beforehand, she'd have practiced. "Just stay close to me and Charity and you'll be fine," she whispered back.

The judge moved toward Charity and Promise. As he ran his hands over Charity's smooth coat, Josie found herself wishing that Charity could enter the class competitively and win a ribbon. She looked gorgeous and stood patiently while the judge examined her.

"Trot them forward, please," the judge instructed.

Josie looked at Ellie. "Just follow me," she said in a low voice. Ellie nodded, a serious expression on her face.

Josie clicked her tongue. "Trot on," she told Charity.

Charity broke into a trot. Glancing around, Josie saw to her relief that Promise had started to trot, too. All around the ring, everyone was watching them. Charity and Promise arched their necks and pointed their toes, as if they were determined to show off in front of their audience. Reaching the fence, Josie slowed Charity down.

"Good girl," she whispered, and then she and Ellie turned the pair around and trotted them back to the judge. When both Charity and Promise halted perfectly, the crowd burst into applause.

The judge smiled. "That's a very well-trained little foal you've got there," he remarked.

Josie blushed with pride as he walked on down the line to look at the next mare and foal.

After all six mares had been examined, the judge asked their handlers to walk them around the ring again.

"What happens now?" Ellie whispered.

"The judge calls people into the center for the ribbons," Josie said. "He won't call us in, because we're not entered competitively."

"Why not?"

"Because this is a class for mares who have had foals," Josie explained, "and Charity isn't Promise's real mother."

They walked around the ring again. The judge watched for a moment and then beckoned the mare and foal in front of Charity into first place. Just as Josie had expected, all of the other horses and ponies were called into the center except for Charity. She wondered whether they were supposed to leave the ring, but then she realized that the judge was waving her over.

"Come on, he wants us in the center, too," she said to Ellie.

The girls led Charity and Promise over.

"If you could just stop here," said the judge, indicating a spot just in front of the other mares and foals.

Josie and Ellie halted Charity and Promise as the judge began to present the ribbons. After giving out the fifth-place ribbon, he took the microphone from the announcer. Josie was surprised. The judge didn't normally address the crowd directly—that was the announcer's job.

"Ladies and gentlemen," said the judge. "I am pleased to announce that the winner of class twenty is number eighty-two, Bluebird's Fire, with her foal, Song Thrush."

The crowd applauded. The judge waited for the noise to die down and then lifted the microphone again. "However, in this class, we have an additional award to give out." He paused, and the steward handed him another ribbon. "This is for Josie Grace's mare, Charity."

A murmur ran through the crowd. Josie was stunned. What? A prize for Charity? She was very confused.

"Charity has been a foster mother for Promise," the judge went on, "the foal who is with her now. As you can see, both mare and foal are in superb condition. In recognition of Charity's contribution to Promise's health and well-being, the organizers of this show have decided to award a prize for best foster mother." He walked over to Josie. "Congratulations, Josie. You have a very special mare, indeed."

"Th—thank you," Josie stammered, taking the beautiful ribbon.

The crowd broke out into cheers. Josie glanced at Ellie. The little girl looked as happy as Josie felt. The other competitors in the ring all clapped and smiled.

"And now, if you'd like to lead the victory lap . . ." the judge said, waving Josie forward.

Her head swimming, Josie clicked her tongue at Charity.

This can't be happening, Josie thought.

But when they trotted toward the corner and she saw all her friends and family clustered beyond the fence, she suddenly knew that it was. Charity had won a ribbon!

"Way to go, Josie!" Anna called.

"Congrats!" Jill and Ben shouted.

Looking into the crowd, Josie saw her mom and dad, their faces happy and proud. The Rudnicks, Mr. and Mrs. Atterbury, and Mrs. Carter were all clapping wildly.

Once the girls and their horses were back outside the ring, everyone crowded around them. "Charity got a ribbon!" Ellie cried in excitement. "Did you see how good Promise was, Mrs. Grace?"

"They both behaved perfectly," Mrs. Grace said.

"And they looked so beautiful," said Mrs. Rudnick, coming forward to pet Promise and Charity.

"Promise loved being in the ring," Josie said. "Did you see her showing off?"

Mrs. Rudnick smiled. "It would have been hard to miss."

"Do you think you'll do more shows with her? Maybe next year?" Josie asked.

Mrs. Rudnick hesitated. "Um . . . no," she finally replied.

Josie felt disappointed. "But she loved it!" she protested.

"We won't have Promise next year, Josie," Mrs. Rudnick said softly.

Josie stared at her. The happiness she had just

been feeling faded at once. "What do you mean?"

"We've decided we're going to sell her." Mr. Rudnick stepped forward and put an arm around Mrs. Rudnick's shoulders. "Promise needs company, and as she gets older she's going to need to be trained and ridden every day."

The news was too much for Josie. "But you can't sell her!" she exclaimed, tears welling up in her eyes at the thought of never seeing Promise again. "You just can't!"

"Hang on, Josie," her mom said quickly. "You haven't heard the full story."

"*We're* going to buy her," said Mrs. Carter.

"What?" Josie said in disbelief

"We're buying her?" Ellie exclaimed.

Mrs. Carter smiled. "Promise is going to be your pony, Ellie. Your dad and I discussed it with Mr. and Mrs. Rudnick and Mrs. Grace last night. You won't be able to ride her for a few years, but that will give you a chance to have lots of lessons. And in the meantime, she can stay in Charity's field, and you can look after her."

Ellie squealed with delight and flung her arms around her mom in delight.

Josie looked at her mom and dad.

"See, I told you, you hadn't heard the full story," her mother said. "And when Promise is bigger she'll move into the stable at the Carters' house."

"So, I'll still be able to see her every day," Josie said, thrilled.

"We were hoping you'd do more than that," Mrs. Carter put in, with her arms around Ellie. "We'd like you and your mom to continue with Promise's training, and, when she's old enough, we'd like you both to break her in."

Josie couldn't speak. She'd always wanted to break a horse in, to get it used to wearing a saddle and bridle, and to be the first person to ride it. "Oh . . . oh, wow!" she managed to say.

"So, you'll do it?" Mrs. Carter asked.

"Definitely!"

Mrs. Rudnick smiled. "I'd love to keep Promise, but I know she'll have the best home possible with you and Ellie, and at least, this way, it means we can still come and visit her." Her eyes twinkled. "And maybe even see you take her in shows."

Josie smiled back, but she couldn't help feeling

slightly sad for the Rudnicks. "Does this mean you won't have horses anymore?"

"No, actually it doesn't," Mrs. Rudnick said.

"We're going to offer Aztec and Inca a home," Mr. Rudnick explained. "Neither of us can imagine the farm without horses and Aztec and Inca need somewhere to retire to. They'll be happy in our field."

"And we'll be happy to look after them," Mrs. Rudnick added. "They're lovely horses—when they're not being pestered by a playful foal, that is!"

Josie sighed in relief. Everything was turning out better than she could have ever imagined.

Jill caught her eye. "I told you it was a perfect day."

"The best," Josie agreed happily.

Three days later, Mrs. Grace and Josie leaned against the gate at Josie's house and watched Charity and Promise standing side by side in the evening sun.

"I still can't believe Promise is really here," Josie said.

"I think Charity likes the company," Mrs. Grace said. "It must have been strange for her being on her own after always having had Faith and Hope to keep her company before."

Josie watched as Charity raised her head and gently nuzzled the foal's fluffy mane. "She's so good with Promise, isn't she?"

"A natural mother," said Mrs. Grace. She turned and looked at Josie. "What would you say to the idea of Charity's actually having a foal?"

Josie gaped.

"I think she'd love it," Mrs. Grace went on. "And the foal could be your project. Once we've trained Promise together, you'll be experienced enough to take over most of the training of Charity's foal on your own. What do you think?"

"I . . . I think it's a great idea!" Josie exclaimed.

"It would mean not riding Charity for a while," her mom warned.

Josie thought for a moment. She loved riding Charity, but it would only be for a few months, and having a foal would more than make up for it. "That's okay," she said. "There are lots of other horses for me to ride."

Her mom smiled and hugged her. "You know, maybe this could be the start of something, sweetie.

Seeing what you've done with Promise, I think you've got a real talent for working with foals. If you enjoy training your own foal, you might want to think about getting a job in horse breeding some day."

"That would be amazing!" Josie said. She'd never really thought about what she would do when she grew up. If anything, she had imagined she might become a riding instructor, but suddenly she realized that, although she loved helping her mom at the riding school, working with Charity and Promise had been the most rewarding thing she had ever done.

She looked at Charity and felt a great wave of love for the dappled gray mare. Everything was turning out so well, and it was all thanks to Charity. She'd become a mother to Promise, and she'd shown Mr. and Mrs. Rudnick that they weren't too old for horses.

But Charity's given me a gift, too, Josie thought. She's shown me what my future may hold.